the SHADOW
PRINCE

The Prequel to Mortal Enchantment

BY
STACEY O'NEALE

ISBN-13: 978-1496193094

THE SHADOW PRINCE

Summary
Every sacrifice has consequences.

Sixteen-year-old Rowan has spent most of his life living among the mortals—learning to control the element of fire, impatiently awaiting the day his vengeful mother, Queen Prisma, will abdicate her throne. When he finally returns to Avalon for his coronation, his mother insists he must first prove his loyalty to the court by completing a secret mission:
Kill Kalin, the half-human, half-elemental daughter of the air court king.
Willing to do anything to remove his mother from power, he agrees to sacrifice the halfling. He returns to the mortal world with his best friend, Marcus, determined to kill the princess. But as he devises a plan, he starts to question whether or not he's capable of completing such a heinous task. And what price he will pay if he refuses?

Cover Designer: Najla Qamber Designs

Editor: Courtney Koschel

Interior formatting and design by Amy Eye: The Eyes for Editing

This novella is dedicated to my mother, Brenda Howell. Thank you for reading all of those stories thousands of times. None of this would have been possible without your love and encouragement.

CHAPTER ONE

A beach bonfire? Now, that's my kind of party.

Judging by the football jerseys and the excitement level of the group, I guess they'd just come from a winning game. They made their way to the shore with their coolers and a beer keg. A few of the guys dropped their stuff, found a good spot, and started digging their pit. Another guy left the group, returning a few minutes later with the baseball-sized rocks he used to encircle the hole. Girls showed up with handfuls of leaves and twigs. After one of them arranged the sticks into a pyramid, there was only one thing left they needed: fire.

They had no idea the flame ignited only because elementals existed in the mortal world. We controlled and maintained the fire element.

One of the smaller, non-jock looking mortals tried several times to spark the flame with a lighter, but the wind coming off the ocean blew it out. The poor guy looked embarrassed, peering over his shoulder at a couple of cute girls in a cluster. I decided to make him look like a hero. Hidden behind a glamour, I kneeled beside him as he made another attempt. I touched the twigs with the tip of my finger, setting them ablaze. The crowd cheered, passing around fist bumps. The scrawny kid walked away smiling, holding the hand of one of the girls.

Mission accomplished.

A chuckle rang out above the crashing waves. I turned around, discovering Marcus, my best friend, in his mortal form. He walked toward me wearing a red cashmere sweater and khaki pants; made me think of some preppy mortal getting ready to board a sailboat. But that was far from the truth. He was a Gabriel Hound—a shape-shifting fire elemental. His kind was created by my mother, Prisma, centuries ago. They were the most dangerous members of our court, controlled by her alone. Marcus, however, didn't fit the mold.

He stood at my side. "Working hard I see."

I hadn't seen him in months. Once he learned to shift, his father ordered him back to Avalon. "What can I say? I'm a workaholic."

"Yeah." He snorted. "I'm surprised to see you haven't joined their celebration." He bowed and said sarcastically, "Your Majesty."

"You know me better than that. I'm a total professional," I said, smirking.

He raised an eyebrow. "Ah, yes. You're completely above partying with the mortals. It's not like you'd *ever* break the rules."

"Never." We were both full of shit. I enjoy removing the glamour every once in a while. It sucked to spend all my time in their world, but never actually being part of it.

"It's for the best, you know. Those poor girls could never resist the beautiful boy with the sultry brown locks," he mocked, reaching out as if he wanted to touch my hair. "And those radiant blue eyes—"

I put him in a headlock. "You're a dick. You know that, right?" I laughed. The mortal girls made it easy for me, but I was always honest. Regardless of how far it went, I never gave them any illusions of a future with me.

Maneuvering out of my hold, he managed to twist both my arms behind my back until I couldn't move. "Nice piercing, by the way. Has your mother seen it?" he asked, referring to the silver barbell in my right eyebrow.

"Why would she?" I kicked his foot out from under him and we both fell. "When has she ever taken an interest in me?"

He chuckled, shaking his head. "You're the sole heir to her throne. I'd say that makes you pretty important."

I may be her only biological child, but she has no interest in passing her crown onto me. The mists surrounding Avalon prevented aging. As long as she remained within its protection, she could remain on the throne as long as she wished. There was always a chance she could be killed, but only another royal family member had enough power to take her out. "You obviously don't know her very well."

He rose, then held out his hand to help me up. "With everything going on," he said, tone turned serious, "how could you possibly feel this way?"

Mother had all but abandoned me in the mortal world. We had no relationship. There was no love between us. "What are you talking about? What's going on?"

"Come on, Rowan. Be serious."

There had been no word from Avalon. No messages from her. I crossed my arms. "I have no idea what you're talking about."

"Your Mother sent me." His eyebrows furrowed as if he were genuinely surprised by my ignorance. "She's abdicating her throne to you."

Total astonishment didn't begin to explain how I felt hearing those words. Part of me was too shocked to do anything but stand there. On the rare times I'd been invited to visit her in Avalon, she'd never once expressed any interest in passing her crown. "What about Valac and Selene?"

"They have no real claim to the crown." Marcus responded.

My older, adopted siblings have always been her favorite. They'd been together for centuries. If she wanted to abdicate her throne, I expected she'd fight to give it to one of them. "None of this makes any sense."

"Who cares *why* she's doing it? I say go with it."

I wasn't naïve. There was a purpose to her decision. She wouldn't hand the court over to me unless she got something in return. Something she couldn't get without my help...but what could it be? "You don't find any of this the least bit strange?"

He let out an exaggerated breath. "I see where you're coming from, but I'm looking at the broader picture," he said, putting his hand on my shoulder. "In a few days, you'll be king. You'll be able to run the court as you please. You can make all the changes we've always talked about."

Mother believes our people obey because she is ruthless. For that reason, she keeps them in constant fear for their lives. There had been severe punishments for the smallest of crimes, along with plenty of violent executions that she seemed to enjoy. But it was the hounds who received the worst treatment. They'd been kept as servants in the castle, the strongest ones assigned to high-ranking elementals as guardians. If I were king, I would put an end to all of it.

"Are you sure she's serious?"

"There's only one way to find out," he replied, shrugging.

Marcus was right. If she wanted something, I had to go back to Avalon to find out what. "So, why did she send you to deliver the news? I assumed you'd be busy training to be a guardian."

"I completed my training," he said, lowering his head. "I am now yours to command."

An ache formed in the pit of my chest. Mother had assigned my best friend to be my servant. She had made it clear she didn't approve of our friendship years ago, but this was going too far. She has done this only to hurt me. "I won't accept this."

"All the more reason for you to return home." His eyes bore into mine with a fierceness I rarely saw in him. "Accept whatever her terms are and be our next king."

The reality of the situation finally set in. If she was for real, I would be the next king of the fire court. Instantly, all my buried fears rose to the surface. "How do you know I won't end up just like her?"

"Because I believe in you."

I had the fate of the entire court resting on my shoulders. My chest tightened, making it hard to breathe. I needed a break from the seriousness and pretended to wipe away a tear. "Should we hug it out?"

"Oh shut up and get moving already." He pushed hard enough to make me lose my balance.

"I wish you could've seen your face, man."

Marcus did his best to hide his smile. "You forget how easy it would be for me to rip your head off."

If it were any other Gabriel Hound, I'd be concerned. They weren't built with a sense of humor. A

misunderstood joke could quickly escalate into a deadly battle. Marcus was a rare exception. He inherited more than his Mother's caramel skin and curly brown hair. His time with her had given him a moral compass unlike his sadistic father. I rubbed my hand over my day old stubble. "And mess up this thing of beauty? What a tragedy *that* would be."

"Yeah, yeah, yeah." Marcus pointed over his shoulder. "There's a pathway about two miles from here. I think we should start making our way there."

I nodded and followed him into the forest. The bright moonlight found its way through the thick brush, illuminating our way. The only sounds were the rustling of leaves and the twigs snapping under my leather boots. "How are things at the castle?"

"I'm sure it's exactly how you remember it," he replied, letting out an exaggerated breath.

During most days, the castle hosted members of the council who were elder elementals acting as advisors, high-ranking knights, and various elementals fighting to gain favor with my mother. No one really trusted anyone, and everyone had their own agenda. I had zero interest in taking part in any of it. But once I was king, they couldn't be avoided.

Fifteen minutes later, we reached the portal. Avalon was located in the middle of the Atlantic Ocean, concealed from the mortals. It was possible for an elemental to travel there by boat, but pathways were the quickest way. Luckily, they were hidden all over the world. The one we were about to use looked a bit like a swirling tornado, surrounded by a ring of fire. It wasn't painful to walk into, but it was pitch dark, which took some getting used to.

I motioned for Marcus to go first. "I'll be right behind you, sweetness."

Marcus rolled his eyes. A second later, he stepped into the abyss.

I took one last glance at the mortal world, not sure when I'd be back. Memories of my childhood raced through my mind. Handed over at birth, I was raised in secret by mortals who worshipped the nature gods. I thought back to the years I'd spent training with other elementals until I could control our element. My life, up to this point, had been fun. Now, on my sixteenth birthday, I'd aged enough to return to Avalon, and unexpectedly, to ascend to the throne.

I felt a bit of hesitation knowing my life was about to change in every possible way. I had never prepared myself for the life of a king. I never thought I'd rule. But mostly I worried about what effect the throne might have on me. Would I become cold-blooded like her? Really, there was no way to predict.

"Time to man up." I took a deep breath, stepping inside the pathway.

The portal opened on the edge of the woodland territory, the scent of cedar filled my nostrils. It has been many years since I last stood in Avalon. The twisted tree trunks reached into the skies. I could make out the mountain ranges in the distance. The darkened skies prevented me from viewing their peaks. The air court castle was on top of the highest mountain, but even during the brightest light, it stayed hidden in the clouds.

We headed in the opposite direction. The farther we went, the more the scenery changed. The greenery lessened until the ground was only a few sparse patches of grass. I soon caught the aroma of ash. I had stepped inside our territory. The land was flat enough to see for miles. It was nothing more than desert, patches of burnt grass, and dead trees. It was hard to imagine that anyone would want to live here. But it was home.

Beneath the dry land, the castle rested inside the core of an inactive volcano. I took off my trench coat. My black-feathered wings released themselves from beneath my skin, stretching until they were at full length. They immediately caught the hot wind blowing all around us and I had the urge to fly. The power of our element was strongest here. Its energy recharged me with each passing second. Closing my eyes, I focused on the vibration humming through my veins.

"How do you feel?" Marcus asked, reminding me he was here.

"Intense." All fire elementals drew their power from our element, but royal family members had a deeper connection. Being part of the House of Djin meant my ability to control fire and physical strength are way above most elementals. I opened my eyes. "I'd forgotten how good it feels to be so close to the eternal flame."

"We should get going," Marcus blurted. "The Queen will be waiting."

He stared into the distance, his fingers tapping the side of his leg. Wild energy was radiating off him in waves. Was he nervous about returning to Avalon? "Is there anything you want to tell me before we get to the castle? Did something happen?"

Gazing into the distance, he replied, "Nothing you need to worry about."

I understood his hesitation. With the exception of Marcus, most hounds stayed with their own kind. Very few were privy to their secrets. But he was like my brother, I could tell when something was bothering him. "I'm not moving another inch until you tell me."

After a long pause, Marcus pulled his sweater over his head. When he turned around, I gasped. Long, bloodied slices were cut into his back. As I moved closer, I noticed faded bruises and scars beneath the fresh marks. There was only one way to get those wounds. "Why were you whipped?"

"They said I needed to toughen up before I could become a guardian," he replied, putting his shirt back on. "It was a regular part of my training."

Rage surged through my body. No one deserved this kind of treatment—least of all, Marcus. "Who's responsible for this?"

"Isn't it obvious?"

Of course, my mother. Fire burned at the tips of my fingers, begging for release. I never agreed with the hounds' position in our court, and soon, I'd have the power to put an end to it. "This is bullshit."

"That is why I didn't want to tell you." He waved his hands in front of him. "You need to forget about it and go in there with a clear head."

This was another example of her brutality. Throughout the years I'd heard of countless times she'd been responsible for much worse. I had hoped it wasn't true, that somehow, there might be some degree of decency left in her. It was time for me to accept there wasn't. "I refuse to let this continue!"

"This isn't your decision." Marcus insisted.

"The hell it isn't." I took a few steps toward the volcano, determined to have words with my mother.

Marcus stood in front of me, blocking my path. "Remember, she doesn't have to abdicate her throne. You could lose everything if you confront her."

He was right. She could be Queen for as long as she wanted. If my mother continued to reign, many more would suffer. I was nauseous thinking of the torment our court had endured. "How can you expect me to accept this?"

"I expect you to do what's necessary to claim your throne." Marcus must have sensed that I hadn't let it go because he let out a frustrated breath. "You can make all the changes you want once it's your court. But for now, you need to play along."

I smirked. "Well, then I guess it's time I go play."

CHAPTER TWO

Home sweet home.

Black obsidian glass covered every inch of the dark, twisted hallways. I ran my fingers down the smooth surface as we made our way toward the throne room. Gold sconces with endless fire lit our path. Although the volcano hadn't been active for centuries, it was always warm in the castle. It reminded me of the Caribbean, minus all the beautiful beaches. The interior walls echoed with an erratic thumping. I wasn't sure where it was coming from, but I had a feeling I'd find out soon.

"Are you nervous?" Marcus asked.

"Nope." I lied. I never knew what I was walking into when I visited my mother. Her moods were unpredictable. I fisted my hands at my sides. I couldn't shake the feeling that she had ulterior motives behind my planned coronation. I had to find out what they were.

Cheers rang out as we approached. Was it a good sign of things to come? Most of the court activity took place in the throne room, anything from greeting guests to punishing those who broke the decrees—universal laws that all four courts obeyed. Two bare-chested, burly knights moved out of the way as we came to stand in front of a golden entrance.

I pushed against the heavy metal door, stepping into

the massive throne room. Inside, dozens of fire elementals stood in clusters. Elementals ranging from over-sized ogres to nasty little goblins. Then, somewhere in the middle, there were the more human-looking elementals like me. None of them turned when we entered; each focused on something in the center of the room.

Hovering above everyone else on a throne made of lava rocks sat my mother, Prisma. Even without her crown, she stood out. Her wavy brown hair hung low down her back. She wore a gown with a strapless red bodice, and a skirt made of black feathers. The feathers likely came from the wings of an unlucky elemental in our court. Noticeably absent were my adopted siblings who were typically at her side.

Mother's light green eyes were wide with excitement as she peered down at something I couldn't see. We fought our way through the crowd only to be startled by what we saw.

Two Gabriel Hounds circled each other. Their sleek black fur covered in bloody gashes and cuts, as if they'd been fighting for a while. Except for their fiery red eyes, they resembled large panthers. The room shook when one of them growled, explaining the noise I'd heard earlier. A second later, the same hound lunged forward. His teeth bit into his challenger's leg, collapsing him to the ground. The hound let out a wail of agony. Marcus hissed.

I glanced at him. "You okay, man?" I asked, noticing the concern all over his face.

He didn't answer.

The hound who delivered the blow strolled away, assuming the fight was over. Big mistake. While his attention was elsewhere, the wounded hound leaped to his feet. He dove on top of the hound, rolling him onto his back. His sharp teeth sunk into his throat, tearing into his skin. My stomach churned. As a puddle of blood grew around them, the crowd inhaled a collective breath. Once the Gabriel Hound shrunk back into his mortal form, it was clear he was dead. He couldn't have been more than a teenager. Rousing applause broke out in every corner.

The winning hound shifted back into a dark skinned, muscular mortal form. He was double the size of his competitor. When he turned in our direction, I realized it was Marcus's father. Fire elementals rushed the stage, stepping over the fresh corpse.

Marcus ran his fingers through his brown curls. "My father has never been beaten."

"I wouldn't want to take him on." I said, trying to lighten the mood.

"Neither would I."

"What is this I see?" My mother's unmistakable voice silenced the room. "Has my son finally returned to me?"

After years of rejection, I'd accepted that my mother wasn't capable of traditional love. She saw love as a weakness. Only the most feared could rule. "I was just enjoying the entertainment," I said, pointing to the trampled corpse. I thought this was completely barbaric. Forcing the hounds to fight to the death was another way to keep them from being seen as equals in our court. "This is quite a welcoming party."

She stood, eyes squinted. "Come closer so I can see you."

Without a word, Marcus joined the group of hounds. His father noticed him, but didn't acknowledge him. The rest of the crowd parted as I headed toward her.

Tension built in my chest as the potent scent of blood and burnt flesh filled the air. Elementals whispered as I passed, followed by winks and seductive smiles. News must have spread that I'd be on the throne soon. Now, they would covet for my attention.

When I reached the bottom of the throne steps, I bowed. "You summoned me, Your Majesty." She insisted I address her formally.

Tapping her fingers against her arm rest, she asked, "Are you happy to be home amongst your kin?"

I didn't see how anyone could truly be happy while living in fear. Once I ruled, I vowed to work toward restoring balance. "Yes, I am."

She sat down, taking a quick glance at the hounds, then returned her attention to me. "I am pleased your new servant was able to return you to court so quickly. Tell me, are you pleased with my selection?"

Bile built in my throat. I had no doubt she was intentionally digging at me, hoping for a negative reaction which would provoke punishment. "I am very pleased. Thank you, Your Majesty."

"Oh, you're quite welcome," she said smugly.

I bit my tongue, hoping it would prevent me from saying something I would regret. Instead of speaking, I smiled at her. The tension in the room was as thick as butter.

After a long uncomfortable moment she rolled her eyes, bored with the conversation I assumed. "There will be a ball at sundown in celebration of your upcoming coronation. You may return to your quarters until then." She pointed to Marcus, a wicked smile across her face. "Your servant will escort you."

Again, she attempted to upset me. No doubt, she'd meant to use this to teach me a lesson. To her, the hounds were little more than animals. Most of them were feral, but because I'd spent time with Marcus, I knew they were also intelligent. She watched me intently for any reaction. But rather than giving her what she wanted, I bowed. "Thank you, Your Majesty. I look forward to the celebration tonight."

"Continue with the games," she shouted to the hounds. The crowd roared with anticipation.

Two more hounds somberly transformed into their animal forms, preparing to fight to the death. My power surged in my fingertips, aching to stop what was happening. But I remembered what Marcus had said about control, and I did nothing. Instead, I tilted my chin toward Marcus. He nodded, quickly appearing at my side. I followed him toward the exit as I tried to block out their pained cries.

I wanted to talk to her about the coronation, but there was no point. There were too many elementals around, she was having too much fun enjoying the blood bath. It would be easier to speak to her at the party tonight. At some point, I was sure I'd have an opportunity to get her alone.

When the door closed behind us, Marcus let out a breath he was holding in. "You handled her better than I thought you would."

Some of the tension released from my shoulders, but the image of the dead hound remained in the front of my mind. "There were a few moments where I almost lost it."

"But you didn't," he said, genuinely pleased. "If you can manage to keep it up over the next week, you just might pull this off."

Being around my mother put me on edge. I needed to change the subject. "Why don't you tell me more about this celebration of hers? Who's going to be there?"

We strolled down the hallway, continuing toward my bedroom. "All of the royal families are expected. The preparations have been going on for days. It'll be a lavish event."

No doubt. My mother would take any opportunity to show off her wealth and power. If all of the families were invited, it would seem she was planning quite a show. It would be nice to see the other court leaders. The royal families were especially reclusive, except for King Taron of the air elementals. I had met him on a few occasions during my childhood. He was friendly. My mother disliked him, but I don't remember an elemental she ever truly cared for.

For now, I'd focus on showing up and continuing with my Oscar-worthy performance. I'd do whatever I had to-to survive this week. The future of my court depended on it. After a few twists and turns, we made our way to my bedroom. Marcus reached around, turning the gold handle on the door, pushing it open. I cringed. I knew he had to play the role of my guardian while we were here—anyone could be watching us at any time—but it still felt weird to have him opening doors for me.

The interior walls of my room shared the same obsidian glass as the rest of the castle with gold sconces hanging on every wall. There were no windows or any living plants. Several zebra skin rugs covered the floors leading to a massive fireplace in the middle of the room. I headed past the adjoining black marble bathroom toward the closet. When I slid the door open, I was surprised to find it was full of clothing.

I smirked at Marcus. "Oh, honey, you shouldn't have."

"You're kidding, right? I'm the last person they'd send shopping."

I chuckled, returning my attention back to the clothes. There were several traditional red robes for the important meetings, a three-piece black suit, dark jeans, shirts in a riot of colors, and an assortment of boots sitting on the floor. "Well, whoever it was did a good job. They are all my size."

He shrugged. "Maybe it was the Queen?"

"Not a chance," I said, shutting the door. My mother was centuries old. If she went beyond Avalon's mist, she would age rapidly until time caught up with her. I imagine she'd be dead in a matter of weeks. There's no way she would age herself for anyone, especially me. "She probably sent one of the younger elementals."

A knock on the door piqued my interest.

The door opened. A young, skinny female hound stepped inside holding a tray of cheese, crackers, and wine. I could tell by the patched-over burn holes on the side of her gray dress that it was old. Her shoes weren't in much better shape. With everything available at her fingertips, I would have assumed my mother would provide better attire for the servants. The little hound kept her eyes toward the floor as she waited for instruction.

I took the tray from her, placing it on the black lacquer nightstand next to my bed. "I can take this. Thank you."

Our eyes met and I smiled. As a hound working here in the castle, I doubted she got many kind words from the other high-ranking elementals. Her cheeks blushed. "Is there anything else you need, Your Majesty?"

"Nope. We're all good."

She took a quick glance at Marcus. Her eyebrows furrowed as if she were confused, then she hurried back out the door.

I sat down on my platform king size bed. Leaning against the white leatherette headboard with my hands crossed behind my head, I asked, "Why did she look at you like that?"

"Because I wasn't staring at the ground waiting for a command from you." Marcus crossed his arms. "If she reports me, I'll be punished."

I shook my head. "I won't allow it."

"Yes, you will. You have to keep up appearances." He sat down on the edge of the bed. "Besides, I should have known better."

"I don't want to hear you talk like that." I sat up. "You'll never be a servant to me. Never."

Marcus held his arms open, smiling slyly. "Now I'm ready for my hug."

18

I chuckled, pushing his shoulders with my fists. "Yeah, whatever."

His eyes settled on the mountain of cheese and crackers. "Why don't you send some of those goodies my way? I'm starved."

I rolled my eyes, sliding the tray across the bed. "When are you *not* hungry?"

He stuffed a fist full of cheese cubes in his mouth. "Hey, it's hard work chasing after you," he responded, voice muffled.

Marcus continued to scarf down food while my thoughts lingered toward tonight's ball. If all the leaders of the courts would be there, I couldn't help wondering if my future betrothed would be one of them. All the high-ranking elementals had their partners chosen for them. It had nothing to do with love or attraction. For us, it was all about forming alliances and gaining more power. My mother hadn't chosen my bride, as far as I knew, but I was sure my opinions had no bearing on her decision.

"Looking forward to seeing anyone special tonight?" I asked.

Marcus swallowed what was puffing out his cheeks in one large gulp. "Well, there could be one person, but I'm not sure if I'll be able to talk to her."

He had never shown any interest toward a female elemental before. They must have met during the months I hadn't seen him. "Why?"

"Ariel is an air elemental."

It wasn't uncommon for elementals to date outside their court. But for some reason, hounds only mated with other hounds. "So, what does that matter?"

He stared down at the small crumbles of food left on

the tray. "My father would never approve. Plus, Ariel's parents have already arranged for her to marry a high-ranking knight in her court. You know it's all about moving up the popularity ladder."

"Well, you can at least tell me what she looks like. Is she hot?"

He glanced up, eyes widened with excitement. "She's gorgeous. Long blond hair and lavender eyes just like the other purebred air elementals."

Something came over him as he spoke about her. It was like he was injected with joy juice. "Damn, maybe I should introduce myself."

He scowled. "You're not her type."

I smirked, patting my hand on his shoulder. "I'm everyone's type."

He threw a cracker. It bounced off my cheek, landing in my lap. "I know there's at least one girl out there capable of seeing through your bullshit and I can't wait to meet her."

I picked up the cracker and ate it. It would be nice to have to work for it for once. I would enjoy the chase. "No way. I'm too loveable."

Marcus coughed. "I think I just threw up in my mouth."

I grabbed the bottle of wine, removed the stopper, and poured two glasses. "You can wash it down with this."

He took one of the glasses. "What are we toasting?"

I shrugged. "Being awesome?"

"To our continued awesomeness," he replied, tapping our glasses together with a clink.

CHAPTER THREE

Damn, I look good.

My normally unkempt hair was slicked back, my face cleanly shaven. I checked out all the rest of my angles in the mirror. Somehow, without ever being measured, the all black suit in my closet fit perfectly. The matching shoes were a bit snug, so I decided to wear my leather boots. I'd rather be comfortable anyway. No telling how long this party would run. They've been known to last for days.

Marcus left a while ago to get changed. He said someone would come to escort me. I had been pacing for hours. At the ball, it would be easy for me to pull my mother aside and get to the bottom of her decision. There was a small part of me holding onto a shred of hope that her offer might be genuine. But the rest of me knew there was much more to her decision.

I had learned not to trust her a long time ago. She would turn on anyone if it benefited her.

As soon as one of the knights showed up at my door, we made our way down the long hallway. The walls vibrated with the sounds of sensual, rhythmic music. The noise level escaladed the closer we approached. My nerves tingled with anticipation. I had never been invited to one of these events. But if it was anything close to the rumors I'd heard, it would be a wild night.

A gust of wind whipped against my face as the doors opened to the ballroom. The room was flooded with black feathered elementals elegantly dressed in a cascade of colors. Candlelit silver chandeliers illuminated the dimmed dance floor. Bodies clung to one another, moving to the beat of the erotic song. Wooden tables lined the walls where groups sat, laughing and drinking from crystal flutes. My eyes roamed the room for Marcus but I didn't see him anywhere.

The music stopped, and a single trumpet wailed.

The crowd turned to face me. I swallowed hard. "Prince Rowan of the House of Djin," an unfamiliar male voice announced. Whistles and claps rang from every corner.

I waved, keeping proper protocol.

The tuxedoed knight was leading me toward my mother's table when my siblings stepped into our path. Valac's appearance never changes. His clothing always was pristine, like it was on a mannequin. Tonight, he wore a suit eerily similar to mine. As always, his slicked back black hair was perfect; not a single piece out of place. His face reminded me of cold stone because he very rarely expressed any emotion. His twin sister Selene stood at his side. Her red, floor-length gown looked like it might have just come from a fashion house in Milan. She glanced at me quickly, smiled, and then returned her attention to her brother.

"Congratulations on your upcoming coronation, brother." Valac said, his voice monotone. "I'm sure you'll make an excellent king."

"Thanks, buddy. It almost sounded like you meant

it." I patted him on the shoulder. "Seriously though, I appreciate your effort."

"He does mean it, Rowan." Selene interjected, playing the mediator as usual. "We both do."

If she didn't worry so much about Valac's opinion, she probably would have been happy for me. Selene has never given me the impression she wanted the throne. She relished in all of the spoils a royal life offered. Mother made sure she had the best of everything. She has always favored my siblings, adopting them both centuries ago after they were abandoned.

Mother told me I was conceived after she was raped. I didn't see how that was even possible considering she was the strongest of all the fire elementals, but even to this day, I have no idea who my father is. From birth, she has treated me like an inconvenience—a pebble in her shoe. Which was why Mother's decision to pass the crown on to me didn't make sense.

I need to speak with her immediately.

"Well, this was uncomfortable. We should do it again sometime in the never future." I circled around them before either had a chance to respond. I spotted Mother's table in the far corner of the room. Her red gown was so tight I couldn't even imagine how she was breathing. Several council members surrounded her. The members were wearing suits with a red shawl hanging loosely over their shoulders to alert every one of their positions. They carried on by themselves, not yet noticing I stood there.

I came to stand directly in front of Mother. "Great party. When do the strippers get here?"

Her eyes examined me from head to toe. It was like I

was having a physical without being naked. "You look ridiculous with that metal pierced into your eyebrow."

Score one for me. "I was wondering when you'd notice. I hope you don't mind, Your Majesty." It took everything I had to hold back the smirk paining to grow across my lips.

"It will be removed before your coronation," she said, eyes squinting. Her tone was all statement, zero request. Man, she seemed even more pissed than I envisioned. I gave myself a second point.

"If it pleases you, I'll take it out." I bowed. *It will go back in the moment I'm crowned.*

"The royal families have arrived. Each has their own table," she said, pointing to the other side of the room. "Go greet each member accordingly." Wow, the love coming from her was deep.

"Do you think we could talk first?" There was a reason she'd chosen to pass on her crown. She never made a move unless it benefited her in some way. I had to find out her motivation.

"There will be plenty of time once you've properly greeted our guests." She shooed me away with her hand.

I could feel her scowl searing the back of my head as I sauntered toward the other regal tables. Without question, I knew where I was heading first. I wanted to meet the air elemental that Marcus had fallen for, Ariel. On my way there, three barely dressed females attempted to wave me over. They clung to one another, swaying to the thumping beat of the music. My body ached to join them, but I didn't have time for any of that.

The air elementals long, rectangular table sat

empty. The group stood in a circle in front of it, talking amongst themselves. Their knights kept watch over them, lined up a short distance away. The air court was the most modest of the four. Nothing about their attire was ever lavish or embellished. For the most part they kept to themselves. Preferring to spend their time in the mountains. The beautiful young female refilling their wine glasses caught my attention. Her blond hair was so light, it was almost white. She had to be Ariel.

I was about to say hello to her when King Taron noticed me. I hadn't seen him since I was seven or eight. It had been one of the few times I had been invited to visit with my mother. After a council meeting, he had found me hiding from Marcus during one of our games. He seemed huge to me back then. I must have looked scared because he bent down each time he spoke to me. That day, he had spent an hour showing me some tricks with his wind magic, even letting me throw fireballs at him. I remember wishing I had a father like him. Or any father for that matter.

King Taron held out his arms and gave me a hug. "Rowan, you've grown up quite a bit since I last saw you." Squeezing my bicep, he said, "I'm impressed."

"Thank you, Your Majesty." I bowed. "It's been almost ten years since I last saw you. How are things in the skies?"

"Always changing." He put his hand on my shoulder. "Speaking of change, congratulations on your upcoming coronation. I have to admit, Prisma's announcement was unexpected. I didn't think she planned to abdicate her throne."

So she never talked to the council about her

decision? I wondered if anyone knew about it, or if this was something she decided recently. "It came as a surprise to me as well."

"I've thought about stepping down myself. My daughter will be joining me here in another year. Once Kalin is fully trained, I may abdicate."

His daughter was a mystery to most elementals. All I knew was that she was a halfling, living with her mortal Mother. "You must have a lot of faith in her."

"She's a very special girl."

Orion, king of the woodland court, patted Taron on the shoulder. The two elementals embraced. They had been close friends for centuries. "We all look forward to getting to know Kalin." He said.

"Thank you for coming, King Orion." I bowed. Although the woodland faeries were known to be playfully carefree, they made the best weapons and were widely considered masters of war. But, since the decrees—the laws we lived by—were accepted centuries ago, there has been no major conflict between the courts.

"We're all happy to be here for such a special occasion." Orion waved over one of the male faeries from his court. "Speaking of special, I had this made for you by our greatest blacksmith." The faerie held out a sheathed sword attached to a leather shoulder strap. "I heard you've become quite the accomplished sword fighter," he said, handing me the gift. "This is a weapon made for a king."

I gripped the handle, releasing the blade from its sheath. Taking a closer look, I realized the curved sword was made of iron—the only metal all elementals were allergic to. Many of the weaker ones couldn't be in its presence without feeling an immense, burning pain. However, the stronger elementals used them as weapons. I stepped backwards a few paces to swing it a few times without endangering anyone. It felt light in my hand. "This is an incredible gift. Thank you very much."

Orion put the sword back in the sheath, then slid the leather strap over my shoulder. "Let's hope you never have to put it to good use."

After introductions to a few other woodland faeries, I excused myself so I could greet the members of the water court. Although they had never given me a reason, I always approached them with caution. Most were still seated at their table, taking in the room. They were likely speaking to each other telepathically, which made me nervous. I'd been told the water queen, Britta, could read the thoughts of other elementals. I didn't want her poking into my head, so I cleared my mind as I approached. Britta was hard to miss. Her wings were made of scales rather than feathers. I especially liked the white henna-styled tattoos on the sides of her face.

I opened my mouth to speak and Britta jolted. The color of her blue eyes faded until there was nothing more than white showing. I'd seen this once before as a child. She was having a vision.

"Thank you for coming, Queen Britta." I said, not sure if she could hear me.

From inside my head, I heard, *"I see trouble for you, young prince. Two possible paths lay at your feet. At the end of both paths, your hands are covered in blood."*

"What do you mean covered in blood? Are you

saying someone will die?" My eyebrows furrowed. "You have to tell me more."

"I cannot. The future is always changing. Outcomes are never certain."

"Can you see who the blood belongs to?"

"No."

My head swirled from all the possibilities of her words. Was I about to hurt or kill someone? Was I going to find someone hurt or killed? Was it *my* blood? I couldn't think straight. And at some point, I had unknowingly walked away from her. I stood alone in the corner of the room with no idea of how long I'd been there.

After my disturbing conversation with Queen Britta, I returned to my mother's table. She sat in the same place, talking amongst some of the high-ranking air court members. When she didn't acknowledge my presence once again, I reached my breaking point. I was done waiting for answers. "Excuse your council, we need to talk."

"What about?" she questioned, coyly.

I wasn't in the mood to play games. "You know exactly what this is about."

She made eye contact with her council members. One by one, they got up and left the area. I saw her say something to the final person, but the music was so loud I couldn't hear what she said. No point in asking either.

"Why are you abdicating your throne?" I asked boldly.

She stood, eyes widened as if she wasn't expecting the inquiry. "Why are you questioning my decision?

STACEY O'NEALE

Most children would be thrilled in your position."

"For the last sixteen years I've barely seen you. Then, out of nowhere, you send Marcus to tell me you plan to pass your throne on to me. Wouldn't that sound suspicious to you?"

She put her hand on her chest as if she was shocked. Always the drama queen. "Are you saying you don't want to be king?"

I leaned toward her, resting my fists on the table. "I'm asking, what's in it for you?"

She didn't budge. Nothing or no one would intimidate her. "It's not for me, dear. It's for the court."

I crossed my arms. "What is it?"

"Before you can take the throne of fire, you must first prove your loyalty to this court."

And, here comes the truth. "How?"

"By killing the halfling daughter of the air court king."

"Kalin?"

CHAPTER FOUR

I sat for a long moment, dumbfounded. "You can't be serious."

She grinned proudly. "I am."

I searched my mind for any reasonable explanation for her request, but came up with nothing. "What did Kalin ever do to you?"

She sat in her chair, tapping her fingers against the arm rest. "These are my terms, Rowan. If you want the crown, you *will* kill her."

My mother has never been rational. Actually, she was crazy most of the time. But this was a stretch, even for her. "What you're asking is far beyond murder; it's treason." It would mean breaking every rule in the decrees. Just considering this warranted my execution. "If you want me to do this, I need to know why."

She leaned back in her chair with a disgusted look. No one questioned her orders. After a minute of contemplation, she said, "I believe Kalin is the next akasha."

An akasha was an elemental capable of controlling all four elements of nature. There had been many over the centuries, but there hasn't been a new akasha since the last one died over one hundred years ago. Many thought they were extinct. "That's impossible. The akasha has always been a pureblood elemental. Last time I checked, Kalin was a halfling."

Leaning forward, she scowled at me. "No one knows why an akasha is born. There are no rules to say it must be a purebred."

I crossed my arms. "Why do you believe she's one of them?"

"Taron has kept her in the mortal world, guarded by his knights since her birth—"

"She's the daughter of a king. I don't think it's unreasonable that he would want her protected." Having no concept of real love, it wasn't a surprise that she couldn't understand why a parent would safeguard their child.

"That's not my only reason," she said, visibility aggravated that I interrupted her. "My spies tell me she's never been trained to control her air element. And, she's never once visited Avalon where her power would be strongest."

The decrees prohibit spying on other courts. Of course, my mother wasn't big on following the rules. Although, I had to admit, what she was saying was unusual behavior for an elemental. We each learned to control our element as children. No exceptions. Taron did seem to be hiding her, but was she really the next akasha? "Okay, let's assume you're right. How does this harm you? Their sole purpose of existence is to keep the four elements in balance."

She rose. "Taron plans to put her on the throne. If Kalin is the akasha *and* the air court queen, it gives their court too much power."

"I get it now. It doesn't bother you that she might be the akasha. You're upset because she's part of another court."

She held up her hand, done listening to me. "I have sufficiently answered your questions. You will kill the Princess or you will not ever sit on my throne. Think it through, Rowan, because this will be your only opportunity."

The magnitude of her request finally started to settle in. "You do realize the coronation is only days away, right? Even if I agreed, there's not enough—"

"Then I suggest you leave immediately," she said, leaving the room before I had time to finish my response.

The voices and loud music ringing out all around me had ceased. All I heard was the rapid beating of my own heart.

After this latest demand, there was no question my mother needed to be removed from power. It should have happened a long time ago. As king, I could erase all the fear felt by the members of our court. I could release the Gabriel Hounds from their positions of servitude. Not to mention, my best friend could be free to be with the girl he was falling for.

But could I kill a potentially innocent halfling to make it happen? Could saving thousands justify the death of one who deserved to live? A person who could be the salvation of our entire species? Then I thought of Taron. The ruler who had been the kindest to me. He was thrilled about his daughter coming to live with him. How could I hurt him in such an unforgiving way?

An ache settled in the center of my chest. There was no right way to handle this situation. Regardless of the path I chose, someone would be unnecessarily hurt by my actions. And, if this was the vision Britta had seen, there would be blood on my hands either way.

I'd reached my decision. Mother had left me no

choice. No matter how sick it made me, Kalin had to die. It was the only way I could rid them of my mother. With the leaders of the courts here, it was probably best I handle this right away.

"Hey, man. You look like you're about to puke. Are you okay?" Marcus asked, breaking me from my thoughts.

The room felt as if it was closing in on me. At some point I'd started panting. "I have to get out of here."

"Wait, why? What's going on?" Marcus asked, concern written all over his face.

I glanced around at all the eyes watching us. "Trust me, you don't want to know." I pushed my way through the crowd, heading toward the exit.

"I'm coming with you," he said, keeping pace.

I increased my speed, hoping he'd take the hint. It was best that he wasn't involved. If I was caught, I would be executed. But if Marcus suffered the same fate, I'd never forgive myself. "You can't follow me."

"That's too bad because I'm coming anyway."

We headed through the exit doors, past the guards, and down the hallway. Once I was sure we were alone, I said, "I get that you're trying to be my friend, but you have to understand, I'm doing the same thing. Please, go back to the ball and have fun."

"Rowan, you're freaking me out right now. I'm not leaving until you tell me what's going on."

We reached my bedroom. While turning the knob, I said, "Fine, I can see you're not backing down, so I'll tell you." Once inside, I took a look around to make sure no one was there. Someone had left a tray of assorted appetizers along with a large jug of wine on the end table. "Remember how I told you Mother would want something in return?"

He was already cringing. "Yeah..."

"I was right. She wants something. Something terrible. Something so bad it will require me to break every rule we have set in the decrees." I poured myself a glass of wine, drinking it in one gulp. "And, if I'm caught, I'll be killed."

"Holy shit. I think I need some of this," he said, taking the bottle out of my hand, drinking until there was nothing left. "Okay, now tell me. What does she want?"

Part of me wondered if this was all a hoax. Maybe she wanted me to get caught and die so she'd have no more heirs. In that case, she'd have a much better chance of passing her crown on to my adopted siblings. "She wants me to kill Kalin, King Taron's halfling daughter."

"Why?" he asked, eyes widened.

I sat on my bed, face buried in my palms. "Because she thinks Kalin is the next akasha. She wants me to kill her before she returns to Avalon and gains her power."

"Even if she was an akasha, she's no threat."

Along with keeping the four elements in balance, an akasha would recognize abnormalities within the courts. I sensed my mother was hiding something. It would explain why she insisted Kalin die without knowing for sure if she was the next akasha. "I know this."

"Are you going to do it?" he asked, rubbing the back of his neck.

I glanced at him, wishing for any other way. I would have sacrificed myself if it were best for the fire elementals. "I have to. If I refuse, she'll never offer me the throne again."

Both of us were silent for several minutes. There was no doubt that Marcus was uncomfortable with the whole idea. Any other hound would've encouraged me. Actually, most of them would have offered to do it themselves. But he wasn't like them. He'd never shared the rage they seemed to be born with. The desire to cause pain wasn't in him.

"I don't think this is right, but I understand why you're doing it," he said, settling down next to me on the edge of the bed. "That's why I'm going to help you."

This was exactly why I didn't want him to follow me. There would be no talking him out of it now. "It's too dangerous."

Marcus raised an eyebrow. "Do you really expect me to let you go off on your own? You're my best friend, man. I won't do it." Then, he smiled. "Besides, I'm your guardian now, remember?"

I shook my head. "Being my guardian doesn't mean putting yourself at risk. Maybe even getting killed."

"I'm pretty sure that's exactly what it means," he said, letting out a short chuckle. "Now, what's your plan?"

I let out an exaggerated breath. "I know Kalin's kept under constant surveillance. We'll need to search the area around her house. Find a place where we can watch her without the knights knowing we're there."

"Then what?"

I stood, facing Marcus.

"I'll kill any guard that gets in my way," I said, pulling the sword Orion had given me out of its sheath. The candlelight made the iron weapon shimmer in the light. "Then I will kill her."

CHAPTER FIVE

Marcus was able to find the spies who'd been watching Kalin. Apparently, this had been going on for quite a while. We learned the halfling was living in Baltimore, Maryland, with her mother. She attended a private high school in the city, recently turned fifteen, and was in tenth grade. There was nothing elemental about her life except she had knights with her at all times. They stayed hidden behind a glamour, even following her into each class.

I'd have no choice but to kill her guards in order to get to her which only added to the disgust I already felt.

After we'd packed weapons and supplies, we left the castle without anyone noticing. The ball was still well under way, keeping everyone busy. Marcus had remained silent since we left the castle. An overwhelming sadness lingered between us. There was no question what we planned to do was wrong. Yet, there was no other option. I hoped I could get this over with quickly. But, regardless, I'd always live with guilt. It had already begun to eat away at me. In its place an empty hole which would never be filled.

There was a portal less than two miles from Kalin's house in the middle of a thick forest. A floating ball of fire illuminated our way as we trucked through the dead, matted leaves covering the winter woodland. The scent of pine filled my nostrils. Each breath made puffy white clouds. The temperature was frigid, but I was always warm. A fire elemental could never be cold.

It was well after midnight by the time we reached Kalin's home. I had expected a house in the city, but she lived on the outskirts of town in a simple brick rancher with a large, wooden back porch. The house was enclosed by forest with no visible neighbors in the surrounding areas. There was only one light on inside.

As expected, an air court knight stood in the backyard. We settled behind a line of tall shrubbery. The knight circled the house several times, but didn't seem to notice us. He had no reason to expect an attack. Ever since the decrees were set in place, the courts had been at peace.

"Are you going to kill him?" Marcus whispered, handing me a pair of binoculars from his bag of supplies.

"No. I want to wait and see what we're up against first." We needed to find out how many guards she had. There would likely be more than one of them inside the house. My goal was to attack when she was surrounded by the least amount of knights. I had skills with a sword and my element, but I didn't want to go in over-confident. These knights were trained, deadly opponents. Although Marcus was only a halfling, he had all the strength and fighting skills of a purebred hound. Knowing he always had my back put the odds in my favor, but I preferred to play it safe.

Marcus sat his bags down. The weapons clinked when they hit the ground. Luckily, the guard was on the other side of the house when it happened. "What's the plan?" he asked.

Break the decrees. Potentially start a war between the courts. Murder. Treason. "We'll stay here tonight and assess the situation."

He scratched the back of his head. "What about tomorrow?"

"I'd like to follow her during the day. There might be a chance we can catch her alone. If we don't get an opportunity, I'll make my move at sundown."

Marcus nodded, but said nothing; his emotional conflict written all over his face. If I could help it, I wouldn't involve him in the killing. Only one of us needed to live with the anguish. It was my burden—my throne. A pain I deserved to live with for what I planned to do.

I jolted when another light came on in the house. We were too far away to see anything. I tried looking through the binoculars, but couldn't make out much. I adjusted the settings a few times until I found the right one. I gazed through the binoculars again and everything became clear. The blinds were open, allowing me to see into the room. A girl stood in front of the window. It had to be Kalin. Goosebumps ran up my forearms. She had her long, wavy hair tied back in a ponytail. Unlike the other air elementals, her hair was red. Her skin was creamy white like porcelain and her eyes were a bit larger, like most elementals. Purebred air elementals had lavender eyes, but hers were either blue or green. All elementals were beautiful, but there was something different about her. Maybe it was her mortal half, maybe something else. Either way, I couldn't take my eyes off of her.

She wore a tight black tank top with what looked like baggy pajama bottoms covered in cupcakes—the mixture of sexy and cute I happen to like. She sat down, elbow leaning on the window sill while her cheek rested in her palm. She appeared to be deep in thought. For once, I wished I had the power to read minds like Britta so I'd know what she was thinking. She wiped beneath her eyes with the back of her hand.

She was crying.

As she opened her window, within seconds, two elementals rushed into her room. Did they think she was leaving? They must've been standing right outside her bedroom door. She startled, then hurried them out. Yeah, she didn't seem at all pleased with their presence. After they left, she paced the room, seemingly mumbling to herself. Privacy was important to this halfling. Closing her eyes, she took a deep breath. She was unnerved by their interruption. By her reaction, I'd say this wasn't the first time they had intruded in her life.

A few minutes later she inserted a pair of earbuds, then scanned through a black iPod. Her head bobbed up and down a few times. Soon, the rest of her body joined in as she swayed to the beat of whichever song was playing. Her eyes closed while she mouthed the words. There was something seductive about the way she moved. I pictured myself standing behind her, our bodies pressed together with my hands on her hips—

Wait, what the hell was I thinking? I was here to kill this girl, not ask her on a date. I shook my head. I must have momentarily lost my mind. It wasn't like I hadn't seen a pretty girl before—they were all over the place.

And lots of girls were hot when they danced. I needed to refocus, or maybe I needed to get some sleep. The last twenty-four hours had been intense.

"What are you staring at?" Marcus asked, taking the binoculars.

I cleared my throat, feeling a bit like a creeper. "Nothing, man."

He stood at my side. Both of us watched her, but only he could get a good look. "Oh, now I see what you're looking at," he said, nudging my elbow with his. "She's pretty."

"I hadn't noticed." I lied. There was no point in talking with Marcus about her. It didn't change what I had to do.

"Yeah, sure," he chuckled.

"Whatever." I didn't know why I tried to hide my feelings from him. He knew me better than anyone else did. Half the time, I didn't have to speak at all. He just seemed to be able to tell how I felt.

"Are you hungry?" he asked, handing me a torn piece of bread and an apple.

My stomach growled. I bit into the bread, which tasted heavenly. "Thanks," I said, mouth full. Within minutes, I'd eaten everything he gave me.

When he was finished eating, he turned around and I followed. During the time I was checking out Kalin, he'd cleared out a spot on the ground and unrolled a sleeping bag. I didn't even know he brought one. "Why don't you get a few hours of sleep? I'll wake you if something changes," he said.

Again, he knew what I wanted without needing to hear it. "I'm fine."

"We both know that's not true. Stop being stubborn and get some rest."

No, I wasn't fine. I expected I wouldn't feel good about killing this girl, but seeing her face brought the guilt to a whole new level. My chest tightened as I pictured standing over her, ready to slice her throat with my sword. Her eyes filling with fear as she begged for her life. Bile built in my throat. I put my hand over my mouth, taking several steps forward. I vomited.

"What's wrong with you?" Marcus asked.

I waved him off. "It's okay. Don't worry about me."

"Yeah, right," he huffed. "You need to tell me what's going on."

I couldn't talk to him about this. I couldn't talk to anyone. Regardless of how I felt, I had to kill her. It wasn't right. It was wrong on every possible level.

Like a mantra, I kept reminding myself what her death would mean to my court.

It would remove my mother's constant threat.

It would free my best friend.

No matter how much I will hate myself, I have to end Kalin's life tomorrow.

CHAPTER SIX

Marcus had let me sleep until she was about to leave for school. He shouldn't have done that. As I rummaged through the bag of food he'd brought, I worried about how the lack of sleep might affect him later on. I chomped on another apple while he packed up our tent. We had to be careful not to leave any evidence of our presence. Once we completed our mission, it was vital that no one could tie her murder back to the fire court.

The very last thing we needed was an all-out war between the courts.

I scanned the back of her house through the binoculars. Then, her curtains opened. Instantly, my mouth was as dry as the Sahara desert. I cleared my throat.

How this girl managed to pass for a mortal was beyond my comprehension. What fifteen-year-old had a pimple-free complexion, perfectly angled facial features, and hair like she just stepped out of a salon? Staring monotonously out her window, she brushed some of her fiery red wavy hair off her shoulders. Every time I looked at Kalin I noticed a sadness about her. Our spies had said she was popular at school with lots of friends. Yet, both times I'd seen her, she appeared so unhappy. It was an interesting contradiction.

In a way, it was easy to understand. She lived in a

mortal world where she would never be one of them. She had to hide most of who she was. In Avalon, she would fit right in. She'd never have to hide any part of herself. As Taron's daughter, she would have been welcomed by her court, but according to my mother's spies, her father kept most of them away. In her situation, I would have been unhappy. There had been times when I'd felt the same, but at least I had Marcus.

I should have looked away as she tucked her white button down shirt into her navy blue pleaded uniform skirt. I failed. Who could blame me? With a curvy-in-all-the-right-places body like hers, she was definitely bringing all the boys to the yard. Hell, I'd be first in line.

"Pass those binoculars over," Marcus said, jolting me out of my thoughts.

"What? Why?"

He chuckled. "I'm dying to know what put that cheeky grin across your face."

I was doing it again. If I told him what I was really thinking, he'd freak out. I couldn't be this attracted to her. I had to find a way to turn it off, or I'd never be able to kill her. This was getting completely out of control. I held the binoculars at my side, refusing to hand them over. "I don't know what you're talking about. I was surveying the area around her house." I lied, pointing to the empty space in her back yard. "All of her guards must be inside."

Marcus raised an eyebrow, signaling I was full of shit. "Yeah, whatever."

I needed to move past this conversation. "We should start making our way toward the pathway. I'd like to get inside the school before she gets there."

"Aren't you afraid they'll see us?"

"My glamour will protect us both." Elementals could see through any glamour with one exception, the royals. It's one of the perks of being a prince. Royal family members had stronger magic. Kalin had a better chance of seeing us, but since she was an untrained halfling, it was likely she was too weak.

"And you're sure Kalin won't sense us?"

Marcus wasn't questioning the strength of my glamour. This was his way of stalling. He didn't want me to do this. I needed to lighten the mood to get his mind off of it. "She won't sense us, but your stench might give us both away." I pinched my nose while I fanned myself with my other hand.

He punched my shoulder. "Dick."

I laughed, playfully hitting him back. "Come on, let's get going." I slid the sword strap over my shoulder, inserting the weapon inside the sheath.

The pasty white hallways of her school were filled with students heading in every direction. A riot of voices rung out over the sounds of metal locker doors screeching open and smacking closed. The coffee scent was strong enough to make me thirsty. I regretted not stopping by a *Starbucks*. I didn't like most mortal food concoctions, preferring the taste of raw foods. But coffee was an exception—or more like a necessity since I was twelve years old.

We stood off to the side where we wouldn't be in anyone's way. The glamour would protect us from being seen, but if we got bumped, they'd feel us. Thanks to our spies, we knew the location of Kalin's locker—twenty feet away from where she stood. The moment she arrived, I watched for her knights. I didn't see any. They must've remained outside. Maybe after they busted in last night she had insisted on some privacy. If that was true, they weren't doing their jobs. They needed to protect her regardless of her need for space. But their mistake would mean I won't have to kill them to get to her. I'd rather take only one life today.

I wished I didn't have to take any.

In a matter of seconds, a gaggle of people surrounded her. More than half of them were guys, which for some reason turned my stomach. I had been right when I assumed she'd be popular. One of the bulkier guys in a letterman jacket put his arm around her shoulder. She smiled, but when she turned her head away from him, she appeared uncomfortable. A burning sensation built in my chest. It was obvious she wasn't interested in this dude. Why wasn't she pushing him away? She was being too nice. I had to put an end to it.

I ignited a quarter size ball of fire in the palm of my hand.

"What are you doing?" Marcus asked, waving his hands wildly.

"Getting rid of a tick." I said, reaching back like a baseball pitcher. I flung the tiny ball of fire right at him, bouncing against his wrist. Perfect shot. He jumped back, shaking his arm wildly. Pulling up his sleeve, he searched for the cause of the sting. There wouldn't be a mark. I only made it hot enough to get his attention.

Marcus stood in front of me, blocking my view. "What the hell was that?"

Me solving a problem. "Didn't you see that?" I asked, pointing over his shoulder. "She didn't want him on her."

"So you threw a fireball at him? Have you lost your goddamn mind? Her guards probably saw that."

Okay, I had to admit, it was pretty stupid. Definitely not my finest moment. "I didn't see any of them when she came in."

His eyes were so wide, they could have popped out of his head. "Regardless, why did you do that?"

"The guy was all over her." I shrugged, trying to make it seem like it wasn't a big deal. "I was doing her a favor."

Marcus stared at me, a look of amazement across his face. After a long, uncomfortable moment, he put his hands over his face. "I can't believe this."

I crossed my arms. "What?"

He shook his head. "You're into her. You're into the girl we came here to kill."

I waved my hands in front of me. "You've lost it, man. I don't even know that chick."

"Then explain to me what just happened."

As he waited for a response, I tried to come up with a logical answer. I thought back to the moments before I threw it. The irritation I felt watching her squirm in his arm. I wanted to storm up there and punch him in the face.

But why? It made no sense. I didn't need to interfere. He wasn't why I came here. My insides cringed.

Was I jealous?

Impossible. I mean, I couldn't deny I was attracted to her—especially when she danced around in those cute pajamas—but I didn't know her. It was for the best anyway. The more I learned about her, the harder it would be to kill her. I'd rather assume she was a horrible person or dangerous like my mother claimed. That way, I was doing the right thing by ridding the world of her.

The bell rang above our heads loud enough to wake a coma patient. The students hurried to their classrooms while we remained where we stood. Marcus looked like he was about to break a sweat. I understood why. I'd been behaving like an idiot. It was about time I was honest with him. "I'm sorry, man. I made a mistake. I guess I've been off the past two days."

He put his hand on my shoulder. "That's why we need to get this done and go home. The longer we stay, the harder it will be."

It will be hard, regardless. I hadn't taken a life before, but I couldn't imagine there was an easy way to do it. Not for anyone with a conscience. And, once it was done, I'd have to live with what I did. "I agree. Let's track her for the rest of the day and hope for an opportunity."

We spent the rest of the morning following her to each class. Mortal courses were mind-numbing. Each teacher taught from a text book using a monotone voice, which made them sound as bored as the students appeared. Kalin paid attention, unlike some of the other students. She wrote notes diligently in her notebooks, never talking to anyone.

Outside of class, she was surrounded by friends. No matter where she went, someone was trying to get her attention. In the hallway, someone told her something that made her laugh hysterically. I smiled. Taking a quick glance at Marcus, he had a wide grin across his face. Her laugh was contagious. The sound was genuine, lighting up her whole face along with it. As the day went on, I found myself hoping someone else would make her laugh so I could hear it again.

Slowly, I was figuring her out. When she was around her friends, she was a bubbly, happy teenage girl. But it was a mask. Her true identity was always hidden. No one knew she would be leaving for Avalon once she turned sixteen. She'd have to forget about her life here and start another with her father. I imagined it would be difficult to leave the life she'd created. It would certainly explain the tears from last night. The sadness she displayed when she thought no one was looking.

It was different for me. Living a mortal life was never a possibility. I wasn't raised with them. My education and training was always with other elementals. So there was never a hard transition for me. It was odd that Taron would allow her to live as if she were a mortal. There was definitely a reason he kept her away from the elementals, but unlike my mother, I wasn't convinced she was the akasha.

Marcus nudged my arm. "She just asked the teacher for a bathroom pass."

How did I miss hearing her? Oh, because I'd lost my focus once again. I needed to get my head out of my ass in a big way. "This might be our chance."

We followed her out into the hallway where two of her guards waited. She held up her hand when they attempted to follow. I pointed down at Marcus's shoes, trying to tell him to walk quietly without actually saying the words. He nodded, making me believe he understood. We crept slowly behind her, stopping when she opened the bathroom door.

I put my head up to the door. "I don't hear her speaking to anyone. I'm going in."

"I'm right behind you." Marcus rolled up his sleeves, revealing his caramel colored forearms—covered in faint scars. They had to be from his months of training.

A quick reminder of why this was so important.

I held up my hand. "No. I'll do it on my own."

He shook his head.

Before he could say anything else, I said, "She's an untrained halfling. I can handle her." It wasn't a lie, but the reason I didn't want him in there was because I didn't want him to be a witness. Without him saying it, I knew he didn't agree. I didn't either, but I would be king. I should be the one to kill her.

I opened the bathroom door inch-by-inch. Kalin was in one of the middle stalls. The toilet flushed. A moment later, she stood in front of the sink with her hands gripping the sides. She stared at her reflection in the mirror. Her expression somber.

This was my moment. I took several steps forward as I slid the sword out of its sheath. With only a few feet of space between us, I was close enough to take in the strawberry scent of her hair. There was another aroma coming off her. Perfume? Something with honey and cloves. I closed my eyes, taking it in.

I put my fist against my forehead. *What the hell am I doing?*

Enough of this stupidity. I gripped the sword with both hands, pulling it back over my head. From this angle, I could decapitate her. There would be no screams for help; she'd be dead in seconds. Sweat pearled in the palms of my hands. My mind raced through the events of the last twenty-four hours. Visions of her laughing, smiling, and dancing. I couldn't get the images out of my head. My stomach twisted in knots. Suddenly, the weapon got heavy. My arms were shaking.

It was as if my mind and body had turned against me.

I lowered the blade to my side. Frozen as I watched her wash her hands. Then she walked out of the bathroom.

Marcus raced inside. "Are you all right?"

I dropped to my knees, letting the iron sword fall to the floor with a clang. "I can't do it. If I kill her, I'm no better than my mother."

He let out an exaggerated breath. "Good."

My head jerked up. I questioned whether I heard him correctly. "How is that good?"

Marcus sat on the floor next to me, leaning against the white tiled walls. "Because I don't want you to kill her. Even if it means I'll never be free. How could I be happy knowing someone as innocent as Kalin died because of me?"

"Why didn't you say something earlier?"

He played with his hands in his lap. "I was being selfish. I kept trying to convince myself that this was okay, but it's not." His eyes met mine. "I was about to bust in and stop you when Kalin walked out. The instant relief I felt assured me this was all wrong."

The decision was made. Neither one of us could justify what we were about to do. It meant sacrificing the crown, but even worse, it meant that Marcus may never be free. But I was sure he was aware of the sacrifice. We both agreed it wasn't worth taking an innocent life. Deep down, I'd known that all along. "I think we should go back to Avalon."

"Your Mother isn't going to be happy about this."

No one refused my mother. There would be severe repercussions for my decision. There was no way around it. "I would rather accept her worst punishment than kill Kalin."

Marcus rose up, brushing off the back of his pants. "You won't do it alone."

I stood. "Yes, I will. You came here as a friend. This was my task. I will accept whatever she dishes out, and if you're my friend, you'll stay out of it."

He lowered his head. "How can I—"

I cupped his shoulder, giving him a light squeeze. "You'll do it for me. We both know she will kill you without hesitation, just to hurt me. The further you stay away from this, the better."

Whatever she did would be brutal, but not deadly. I had rejected her order. But I was her only son. If she truly planned to abdicate her throne, she may not want to kill me now. As I thought about it more, I hoped I was right, but the uncertainty lingered. Mother was unpredictable. She could decide to make an example out of me.

It was time to find out.

CHAPTER SEVEN

Within hours, we were back in the fire court castle. The dark obsidian hallways were quiet for once. The only noise was our boots clicking against the rock flooring. Our pace was slow as we made our way toward the throne room. I wasn't sure what I would say to Mother.

Beyond saving Marcus and myself, I still had concerns about Kalin. I couldn't kill her. Neither could Marcus. But that didn't mean Mother wouldn't send someone else. There was a chance she could convince another royal in one of the other courts to help her. I had to show her Kalin was no threat. And, based on what I saw, I didn't believe she was the next akasha. There was too much mortal in her.

Honestly, I doubted she had any elemental powers at all.

Once we reached the door to the throne room, I stopped Marcus before he entered. "I don't want you to say anything. Let me handle this."

"All right," he said, hesitation in his voice.

"I mean it. Regardless of what I say, or what happens, you go along with it. I don't want you to be punished."

"Be careful. Remember, this isn't the time for your usual sarcasm."

He knew me too well. "I know."

A gust of wind blew into my face as the doors opened. At least a hundred elementals, including a few council members and their guardians, filled the room. They were scattered in clusters. As expected, Mother was sitting on her throne. My adopted brother and sister stood on either side of her. All three of them turned to us as we stepped inside.

Mother remained sitting, tapping her fingers on the arm rest of her throne. "Have you completed your mission, Rowan?" she shouted.

We came to stand in front of her at the bottom stairs leading to her chair. I bowed. "No, Your Majesty."

Her eyes widened with surprise. "Then why have you returned?"

"I cannot complete the task you've given me." The silent room filled with sounds of faint whispers. Each of them had been around long enough to know what would happen next. There was no room for failure in my mother's court.

"Are you refusing my order?"

"I've spent the last twenty-four hours watching the girl carefully. Based on what I've witnessed, I do not believe she is a threat to anyone."

Mother rose and made her way down the stairs. Only inches away from my face, she said, "I did not ask you to *spy* on the girl."

"No, you didn't." I responded with barely more than a whisper. I didn't know why Taron kept her hidden, but if I revealed what Mother thought she was, some may seek her out to see for themselves. Or, they may fear Kalin as she does. Regardless, I wouldn't put her in any danger. "You asked me to break one of the sacred rules of the decrees. To commit treason. To murder a royal family member. I'm sorry to disobey you, but I cannot do what you have asked of me."

She circled me. Speaking loud enough for the crowd to hear, she said, "I asked you to prove your loyalty to this court. To show me you are worthy of my crown."

"I have shown I am worthy by making the right choice regardless of the consequences."

She placed her hand on the side of my face. From anyone else, it would've been a sweet gesture. From her, it wasn't. "Well then, are you ready to accept my judgment?"

I put my hand on top of hers, removing it from my face. "Yes, I am ready. But I ask that you spare Marcus. He had accompanied me with the intent to help me complete my task. It was my choice to refuse your command."

She let out a chuckle. "Very well. Marcus will not be punished."

"Thank you, Your Majesty," I said, trying to sound as genuine as possible.

"I wasn't finished," she said with a wicked grin. "Marcus will not be reprimanded. However, he will assist in your punishment."

I glanced at Marcus, then back to Mother. "What do you mean?"

"I'll show you." She pointed at Marcus.

He dropped to his knees, pained screams echoed the walls. She was using her power to force him to shape-shift into his hound form. I clenched my fists at my sides. "This isn't necessary. You don't need to do this."

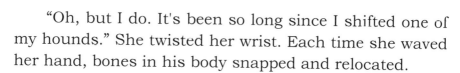

"Oh, but I do. It's been so long since I shifted one of my hounds." She twisted her wrist. Each time she waved her hand, bones in his body snapped and relocated.

Marcus clenched his teeth, trying to hide the pain. I agonized next to him, knowing there was nothing I could do to help. She wouldn't stop. Not even if I begged. She was hurting him to punish me. To cause me pain.

It was working.

Standing on all fours, he had already doubled in size. Clothing ripped from his growing torso until there was nothing left but shreds of fabric around his feet. Coarse black hair grew over his caramel skin. As he growled, his face morphed into something resembling a panther. Hands became paws until I could see nothing mortal in him.

She stood back to admire her work. "There. Now isn't that better?"

Marcus let out a howl, shaking the room. I lost my balance, almost falling. He couldn't communicate while in his animal form, but when we made eye contact, I could see his fear. I bent down, putting my hand on top of his head. "I'm so sorry. I will get you out of this, I promise."

Two guardians in mortal form appeared at my sides. Each gripped one of my arms, pulling me into a standing position. I attempted to fight my way free. But breaking their hold was like trying to break free from iron chains. I didn't budge an inch. "What is this, Mother? Am I one of your prisoners now?"

She addressed the crowd. "Let this be a lesson to all of you. I will not tolerate disobedience in my court. If you refuse me, you *will* suffer the consequences."

I glanced down at Marcus. Whimpering, he stepped toward me, then moved back. When I turned to look at Mother, she was holding out both of her hands like she was trying to control a puppet. The elementals around us cheered. They enjoyed watching the tug-of-war as Marcus fought for control of his own body. Whatever she wanted him to do, it was clear, he didn't want to do it.

I tried pushing my body weight into one of the guardians, hoping he'd loosen his grip, but nothing happened. These two hounds were immovable. Tears welled in Marcus's eyes. My chest ached imagining how much pain he was in. I had to stop this. "Stop fighting her, man. Let her do what she wants. You promised me, remember?"

"I will take my retribution," she shouted over the roaring horde.

Taking a defeated exhale, Marcus settled behind me. The guardians pulled my sheathed sword over my head and removed my leather jacket. Someone from behind tore my t-shirt off. My wings protruded out of my back, expanding across my shoulders. "What the hell are you doing?"

I had my answer as soon as I felt Marcus's teeth sinking into one of my wings. I screamed out as I tried to fight my way free. Was this really happening? Searing pain ran down my back each time his claws tore through my flesh. As his jaws clamped down, I heard bones breaking like microwave popcorn. With each snap, stabbing pain radiated between my shoulders in waves. As he shook his head back and forth, the skin and cartilage connecting my wings to my back separated. Bloodied feathers fell to the ground in clumps. With a thud and applause from the crowd, my wing landed at my feet.

My knees buckled from the injuries and blood loss. The guardians held me in place as Marcus repeated the same process on my other wing. At some point, I went into shock. The world around me was silent and I wished for death. My eyes were half closed with starbursts in the corners of my vision, yet I managed to lift my head high enough to see my brother smiling. My sister had her eyes closed and arms crossed, face turned away from me. Regardless, neither of my siblings moved or attempted to help me.

The guardians released me. I flopped on the ground, landing right on my face with a loud snap. Coppery blood dripped from my nose into my mouth, making me gag.

My nose.

My wings.

Everything was broken.

I was broken.

What a fool I'd been. All these elementals I had hoped to rescue from my mother celebrated as I was mutilated. Not a single one of them tried to stop what was happening or begged for mercy on my behalf. This court wasn't worth saving. None of them.

Except Marcus.

As I lay here, possibly dying, my heart broke for him. If I lived my scars would heal, but he'd have this memory for the rest of his life. And if I died, he was the one who killed me.

I turned my swollen face to the side, resting my

cheek on the cold floor. I couldn't open my eyes. I didn't know where Marcus was, but I hoped he was close enough to hear when I whispered, "It's okay."

"Get him out of my sight," she ordered.

There was a discussion going on above me. My heartbeat pounded in my ears making it hard to hear what they were saying. It sounded as if they were trying to decide what to do with me. Someone mentioned the dungeons. Another suggested throwing me out of the castle. It didn't matter to me anymore. I'd been left for dead by my own family. My court had abandoned me. What was left?

Then, there was nothing.

CHAPTER EIGHT

I had no sense of time. For a while, black emptiness was the only thing that surrounded me. It was peaceful. Painless. Comforting, like I was meant to be there. I awoke abruptly as someone carried me away. My eyes were at half-mast, but open enough to see I'd been flung over the back of a coarse haired creature. A hound? Whatever it was, it travelled at a rapid pace. The constant movement aggravated my wounds until every inch of my body ached. If I had any energy left, I would have let out a pained scream.

The world melted away into black again, but this time, the pain remained. We must have entered a portal. Within minutes, a flash of light. I opened my eyes as someone took me up a steep hill. Heavy winds blew around us. The air was cool and crisp. Then came the panicked voices. They rattled in my ear. Some I recognized. Others I didn't. I heard my name several times, and I wanted to answer, but I didn't have the strength.

They removed me from the animal, stretched me across a tan, flat surface. I ended up in a room lined with beds and wooden cabinets. It resembled a recovery room in a mortal hospital. Except, there were no mortals here. All the wheat blond hair and lavender eyes crowding the room told me they had taken me to the air court. More than likely, their castle on top of Avalon's highest mountain.

They had splayed me across one of the beds. I laid on my stomach. It was only moments before some of my blood trickled down on their lemon scented white sheets. Air elementals hurried, mixing herbs, retrieving cloths and bandages. I'd never seen them so panicked. It was safe to assume my injuries were worse than how I had imagined them. If they looked as bad as the pain I felt, I was in big trouble.

Then, it was as if someone pressed pause. All the elementals stopped moving. Each one bowed their head. A member of their royal family must have entered the room. One set of footsteps clicked on the floor. The sound got heavier as they moved in my direction. My head was turned the opposite way, making it impossible to look. I tensed when a warm hand touched my shoulder.

"Rowan?" a male voice asked. It only took me a second to realize it was King Taron. "How did this happen?"

A female elemental stepped forward. "We don't know, Your Majesty. He came through the portal unconscious on the back of a Gabriel Hound. He hasn't spoken since he arrived."

It was Marcus. It had to be.

"Everyone leave us," he demanded. In less than a minute, the room had emptied. "I don't know who did this to you, but you will tell me when this is all over. For now, I need to tend to your wounds."

The air elementals were the best healers among all the courts. Taron had a very special ability. He could heal others without the need for herbs or other potions. It was magic only members of his kin could perform. It wasn't commonly known. I had told Marcus once about his special power. Clever thinking to have brought me here.

Taron brushed a finger around the edge of one of the gaping holes in my back where my wings had been. "Who would do such a thing?" he asked. I wasn't sure if he was speaking to me or to himself. "Rowan, if you can hear me, you were brought here without your wings. There's no way for me to create new ones for you. However, I can heal most of the wounds on your back."

A warm sensation radiated from my back. Muscles tightened. Skin pulled, closing together. It was excruciating. I needed to concentrate on something else, anything to not focus on what was happening. I thought of Kalin dancing around her room in her cupcake pajamas. The way she moved. The sound of her laugh echoed in my head. Slowly, the pain faded as if I'd been given a pain-killer. Exhaustion overwhelmed me. I didn't fight it, letting my eyes close.

I awoke some time later. Still in the bed, I was resting on my back in a reclined sitting position. Someone had wrapped my torso in white bandages. I rubbed my eyes. In the corner of the room, Taron sat silently on the edge of his seat as if waiting for me to say something. There was no question, he had saved my life. He, along with Marcus, I assumed. No other hound would have risked their life by bringing me here.

"Thank you," I said, voice raspy from dryness.

Taron got up, poured me a glass of water, and

cupped my shaking hand around the glass. "You lost so much blood, I wasn't sure if I could save you."

I wasn't a member of his court. If he wanted, he could have easily let me die. "But, you did. I am forever thankful."

"The damage to your back was the worst I've seen. You will heal, but your scars will be severe. And, your wings—"

"Gone. I know." The ultimate punishment from my mother. I would never fly again. Never feeling the cool air against my face, the wind tingling through my feathers. For the first time in my life, I truly and completely hated her.

Taron crouched down at my bedside. "I need you to tell me everything."

I wasn't sure I could. Yes, my own mother had forced my best friend to nearly kill me while elementals cheered in support, but could I betray them? Regardless of what had happened, I was still a fire elemental. Tension built in my shoulders. Could I tell him my mother ordered me to kill his daughter? If I told him everything, I would risk starting a war between the courts. Elementals who had nothing to do with this would die. There was no way he would let this go unpunished. Mother had broken too many decrees. Although she'd been forgiven for many heinous acts, this could not be pushed under a rug. To Taron, it couldn't get any more personal.

I tried to take a sip of the water, but when I thought about everything that had happened my throat tightened. My voice was coarse as I said, "I disobeyed an order and I was punished."

He leaned back, eyes wide with surprise. "Prisma ordered this?" he asked, pointing at my bandages. "I don't understand."

Of course he couldn't understand. There would never be a circumstance where he'd order his own child to be punished so severely. He loved his daughter, as a parent should. He protected her, as a parent should. My mother didn't understand love. There was no compassion for others in her. Not even for her own child. "Maybe it's better that you don't," I replied, looking away.

He put his hand on my ankle. "I need to know what happened. I feel like you're hiding something from me."

I was. Something so terrible and unforgiving that I wasn't sure I could admit to it. But I couldn't help wondering if Kalin was still in danger. There was a good chance Mother would send someone else to finish the job. A royal could only be taken out by another royal, but because she was a halfling it might be possible for someone outside the families to kill her. A cold chill raced through my veins. Had Mother assumed I would be brought here? Would she have sent an assassin while they were busy tending to me?

My stomach sank.

No, I couldn't let that happen to Kalin.

Once the words came out, I'd never be able to return to the fire court. But I couldn't live with myself if something happened to her. I swallowed hard, then said, "I think Kalin may be in danger."

He flinched as if he'd been punched in the face. "What?"

"My mother believes she's the next akasha. She sent me to kill her." A numbness settled in my chest as if a piece of me had died. With those words I had turned on my own mother. My court. There was no turning back now. The damage was done. "She insisted I do it before my coronation, but I couldn't. I knew it was wrong. That's why I was punished." I pointed to the doorway. "You need to send knights to protect her. I'm afraid Mother will send someone else to do what I refused to do."

I took in a long breath then slowly exhaled. There was a part of me that felt better. He had to know his daughter was in danger. Taron had been so kind to me over the years. Much more than my own family. For that, and many other reasons, I owed him the truth. But, what he did with the knowledge was out of my hands. I was sure he'd do everything to protect Kalin, but how would he deal with my mother? What cost would my court pay for her poor decisions?

His face turned cold as stone. It was as if someone had flipped the switch from friend to king. "You made the right choice by telling me the truth. I will make sure you receive no further punishment."

I shouldn't have pitied her. Mother deserved whatever she got, but I couldn't help it. Regardless of how awful she had been, she was still my only family. "What about my mother?"

Without any show of emotion, he said, "The council will decide her fate. How many others know about this?"

"Only my adopted siblings." I had a bad feeling things were about to get really rough. After all he'd been through, there was no reason to involve Marcus any further. He'd never tell anyone what he knew. I trusted him completely.

He stood. "Very well."

As far as I knew, nothing like this had ever happened in the history of the elementals. Sure, we have had our problems before the decrees, but no one had ever ordered the death of another royal child. Mother had committed the highest level of treason. She could be put to death for her crimes. "What are you going to do?"

Taron made his way to the door, standing directly under the frame. Waving at someone in the hallway, he said, "You need to focus on your recovery. I'll take care of the rest."

A moment later, he was gone. Yeah, it was about to get real around here. Taron controlled himself, but he was pissed. I didn't blame him. Mother had threatened him in the worst of ways. Over the centuries, he had considered my mother an ally. Maybe even a friend.

Several female air elementals entered my room. They carried wash clothes and bowls of water. Diligently, they worked to remove the dried blood and cleaned whatever injuries Taron wasn't able to heal. There wasn't much I could do except sit and watch. I didn't have the strength to move or complain. I wanted to go after Taron to find out his plans. But that wasn't happening.

I could only pray he wasn't too late to save Kalin.

CHAPTER NINE

Two days had passed without Taron returning to my room. Thanks to the healing herbs my energy was returning. I was walking around without assistance, but the healers wouldn't allow me to leave my room. I was told there were guards outside my door for my protection. I guess I should have expected as much. Once Mother learns of my betrayal, I won't be surprised if she sends knights to try to kill me.

My mind swirled with questions. I needed to know what happened to Kalin. Was she attacked by someone in my court? What punishment had my mother been given from the council? Had anyone hurt Marcus after he saved me? I thought about it for hours and hours until it drove me nearly crazy. I barely ate, sleeping only a few hours at a time. It was infuriating being locked in here, even if it was for my own good.

I sat up in bed when I heard chatter from the hallway. The guards in front of my door moved to the side. Taron stepped inside wearing his yellow council robes. His long blond hair was tied back in a low ponytail. He was both intimidating and regal at the same time. The dark circles under his eyes gave me the impression he hadn't slept much either. I didn't say a word as he sat in a chair directly across from me.

He kept his back straight, maintaining his regal

demeanor. "As you may have guessed, the last two days have been quite eventful." His voice remained as cold as the last time we spoke.

Nerves filled me. I wanted to blast him with questions but it seemed like patience would be best. I wasn't sure where our friendship stood after my revelation so I chose to tread lightly. "Yes, I figured as much."

His eyes bore into mine with a seriousness that made me squirm. "I'm sure you have questions. Let me see if I can answer them. To start, Kalin wasn't hurt. She remains in the mortal world, unaware of what has transpired. More guards have been placed around her home to ensure her protection."

"You're not going to tell her about any of this?"

"No. She will move here in less than one year. I don't want her to feel her life is in danger. I'd rather she enjoy what time she has left in her mortal life."

This didn't seem right. His knights were certainly competent enough to keep her safe. She deserved to know the truth. I didn't agree with his decision, but I wasn't in any position to question him. I moved on to another topic. "And my mother?"

His fists clenched until his knuckles turned white. Only days ago he discovered his only daughter's life had been threatened—by her. "She was taken into custody by the council. She will be executed for treason."

The words turned my blood cold. A part of me expected this outcome. But it was something else entirely to hear the words. "When will this take place?"

Without hesitation, he replied, "This evening at sundown. Immediately after, you will be crowned."

"A public execution?" It was like someone splashed a bucket of cold water on my face. This meant I would have to watch my own Mother's death. Thanks to my coronation, it might seem to others that I was a participant. My stomach churned as I envisioned ripping a bloodied crown off her head and placing it on my own.

"Due to the nature of Prisma's crimes, the council has decided that these events will be stricken from our records. No one needs to know the circumstances of her death or her allegations against my daughter. This could cause civil unrest. Wars with one court pitted against another. No, we need to keep the peace at all costs. The elements must be kept in balance."

He wasn't wrong. The courts agreed upon the decrees for this very reason. If the elements were to unbalance, it could cause natural disasters all over the mortal world. It could ultimately destroy it. As the protectors of nature, we had to ensure this never happened. "What about my adopted siblings?"

He crossed his arms. "They will not be punished. After the council investigated, it was determined they played no role in Prisma's plans."

They didn't participate, but they weren't against it either. Throughout my life they had always agreed with Mothers' every move. However, I didn't feel comfortable saying anything negative about them to Taron. If I did, he would likely have them executed along with her. I worried they might retaliate. But I couldn't justify threatening their lives over something they hadn't done...yet.

As soon as I entered the castle basement I wished I hadn't come. The stained cement walls echoed the sounds of dripping water. The air stunk like it was made of sweat and dirt. This place didn't fit with the typical images of the air court. To me, the air elementals had a quiet, peaceful beauty about them. Nothing like this dank dungeon.

One of the knights led me to a cell with an iron door. Simply touching the door could burn our skin, charring it down to the bone. For that reason, I stood back as the knight used a key on his belt to open the door. Once I entered, I blinked twice to make sure I had seen correctly. Mother sat on a metal chair in the center of a very small, square room. Her red dress had been torn in several spots. Her hair had been pulled back but pieces had loosened around her face. Iron handcuffs covered her wrists with dried blood around the edges. By her appearance, I'd guess she put up a fight before they brought her here.

There was nothing inside her cell. No bathroom. No bed. No food. There was just her, glaring at me with a look of total disgust. It wasn't the first time I'd seen that expression. The only time she ever smiled was when she was inflicting pain on someone else. Yet, even with everything that happened, my heart pained to see her in there. How I still managed to care for her I couldn't understand—I doubt I ever would.

"Have you come here to brag?" She chuckled. "All hail the fire court king!" she shouted, lowering her head in a mocking bow.

I thought long and hard about kicking her in the face. "Honestly, I'm not sure why I came. You certainly don't deserve my sympathy."

"Does this have to do with your punishment, Rowan?" she asked. "Judging by my current state, I'd say I went lightly on you." Leaning forward, eyes squinted, she said, "I should have killed you when I had the chance." She lunged for me but the iron chains around her wrists held her back. They sizzled when she moved. It was the first time I'd ever heard her whimper.

The pain must have been intense because it seemed to calm her down. "You are here by your own doing, Mother. You have no one to blame but yourself."

She rolled her eyes. "I did what was best for my court. That's what a ruler does. We make the hard choices others can't make."

Anger boiled in my chest. "Like choosing to mutilate your own son? Was that one of your hard choices?"

She straightened her back, looking quite proud. "You were weak."

I clenched my fists so hard my fingernails dug half moon crescents into my palms. "You wanted me to kill an innocent halfling."

She stood, ignoring the iron as it burned her skin. "She is a danger to us all."

I took several steps until our faces were only inches from one another. "You don't know that. This is all based on your own opinions. There's been no sign that she's the akasha."

"You're a fool. You refuse to see what's right in front of you." She shook her head. "You will bring doom to our court. I'm pleased I won't be here to witness it."

"You know, I came down here contemplating whether or not I would beg for your life. Even after all you've done, there's part of me that will always care for you. Some small piece of me will always yearn for your acceptance, your love." Tears welled in my eyes but I refused to let them go. After all she had taken from me, I would never give her the satisfaction. "But now I see you are beyond saving. You deserve what's coming to you."

She laughed. "Only the weak yearn for something as frivolous as love. You aren't worthy of my approval. Certainly not my crown."

Her hateful words stabbed into my chest. She never touched me, yet I was beaten and broken. In that moment, I bundled up all the emotions I felt for her and locked them away. Never again would I let anyone get to me as she had. "And yet, here we are. You are about to be put to death, and me, about to sit on your throne." I grabbed her face, pressing my lips hard against her cheek. "Goodbye, Mother."

CHAPTER TEN

This wasn't how I imagined this day would go. My coronation was supposed to be a celebration, the greatest day of my life. The fire court throne room should have been filled with fire elementals and high-ranking members of the other three courts. During the ceremony I'd kneel before my mother. She would say a few words then place the crown on my head. Afterwards, we would party for days honoring this significant moment in our history.

Instead, I sat on the edge of the bed in the guest room of the air court castle. There were no members of my court with me. Only three would witness my coronation: Liana, my mother's sister, and my adopted siblings. The rest of my court would hear about it once they learned of my mother's execution. There would be questions from many, but only a few would know the truth. As Taron had said, none of the records would reveal the details of her treason. The remaining council members felt this was the best way to keep the peace.

Staring out the window I watched the sunset. A purple hue filled the skies around the castle. It was incredibly beautiful. I wore my formal red ceremonial robes that Liana had brought to me. Underneath, my sword was strapped to my back, resting in its sheath. Carrying a weapon wasn't typical for this type of ceremony, but it made me feel safe. Against my mother's wishes I'd left the barbell in my eyebrow. It really didn't matter. Her death would come before I was crowned.

I stood when I heard a knock on my door. A knight handed me a letter, then exited.

Rowan,

I know this is a big day for you and I'm sorry I can't be there. ~~But after everything that happened~~. After what I did to you. The pain I caused. I can't even look at you. I need some time alone to deal with everything. Don't look for me. That will just make things worse. I don't even know what more I can say right now. I'm sorry.

Marcus

I growled. Crumpling the note in my hand, I set it on fire. He was the one person who I could count on, and now, he was gone. He didn't want me to find him. I didn't know for how long. Maybe forever. And there was nothing I could do about it.

Something about his words felt permanent, as if I'd lost my best friend.

I was still reeling from Marcus's letter when another knight came to escort me downstairs. The design of the air court throne room didn't look anything like my court. The rectangular room was massive. Flags with the air court symbol hung high along the cathedral ceiling. White pillars lined the walls with limestone statues of elementals. My boots clicked on the marble flooring as I made my way toward Taron. He sat on a throne made of clear crystal. It was the same stone used on the outside of the castle.

Air elementals in traditional yellow robes made up

the audience. They stood in small groups, whispering as I passed by. I couldn't blame them. They knew my mother was being put to death. I must have seemed like a monster coming to watch. If I had a choice I wouldn't be here. The thought of any execution disgusted me, even more so because it was for my own Mother. But I kept my emotions in check, walking face forward as if I wore horse blinders.

One of the knights led me toward a chair near the king. There was an area cleared out in the center of the room. Within the space was a wooden chopping block and an iron axe. Since they planned to behead her the execution would be quick. Her suffering minimal. After all the hateful things she had said to me I shouldn't care about her pain, but I did.

In the far corner Liana leaned against a wall in her formal red robes. A single tear ran down her cheek as she glared at the execution area. She hadn't been close with my mother, but she was still her sister. Glancing around the room I searched for my siblings. I didn't see either. Perhaps they had chosen not to attend? I wasn't surprised. They had always been closest with my mother. If *I* found this event horrifying, it must be intolerable for them.

The whispers ceased as they brought Mother into the room. There was an air court knight on either side of her. She had cleaned up since I last saw her. Her hands were still locked in iron cuffs, her hair had been braided down her back, and her torn red dress replaced by a thin white gown. With her pale skin she looked innocent and ethereal. It wasn't until she glared at me with her eyes filled with hate that I truly recognized her.

The crowd parted, making a pathway for the knights to take her to the make-shift guillotine. As she knelt in front of the wooden chopping block, she kept her focus on me the entire time. I forced myself not to look away even though my insides twisted into tight knots. She expected me not to watch. To be weak. But I refused. An executioner, wearing a black mask to cover his face, came to stand at her side with the axe in hand. He glanced up at Taron, awaiting his command.

Taron stood. "Do you have any last words, Prisma?" he asked.

Mother remained silent.

"Very well," Taron replied, waving his hand at the executioner.

He nodded, raising the axe over his head.

I inhaled deeply, forgetting to let it out. It seemed as if I had slipped into a dream. Everyone around me was motionless. I was numb; I couldn't move even if I wanted to. Why had it come to this? All of it could have been prevented by mother expressing her concerns to the council. Now, because of her foolishness, I had to watch the only parent I'd ever known die.

The executioner swung the axe, but instead of taking off Mother's head, it sunk into the chest of the closest knight. A cloaked woman ran to my mother. She gripped the cuffs around mother's wrists. Fire burned out of her hands, melting the iron shackles. Her hood dropped back—Selene. Other fire elementals hidden under yellow robes blasted balls of fire into the crowd. Screams erupted as panic ensued.

"Guards," the king shouted. Knights raced in from

every doorway with blades raised. Within seconds, Taron was gone; taken to safety using a hidden doorway.

During the mayhem the executioner pulled a knife out of his side pocket, slicing the neck of the closest knight. I knew it was Valac before he ripped off his mask. Selene wouldn't have done this without him. My fists clenched at my sides. This was his idea.

He helped Mother to her feet, then shot a line of fire into the crowd, creating a pathway to one of the exit doors. They both took one of her arms over their shoulders heading toward the exit.

No way was I going to let this happen. Rage overtook me. My fingertips ignited into burning flames. I flung my robes over my head, the cloth catching fire. By the time it reached the ground all that was left were shreds of charred fabric. I unsheathed my sword, pushing my way through the crowd. One of the fire elementals stepped in my way. A ball of fire formed in each of his hands, but before he could throw them I plunged my iron sword into his belly. His skin seared, still smoking even after I pulled back. He collapsed onto the ground.

I ducked as an air elemental used her wind magic, flinging her attacker into the adjacent wall. Swords scraped against one another while pained cries filled the room. I put my hand over my mouth; the air reeked of burnt flesh. I couldn't see my siblings but I didn't stop shoving my way forward. A male fire elemental cornered a cowering air female. He was about to burn her when I sliced my weapon into the side of his neck, partially decapitating him. Blood smeared across my blade, lightly splattering my face. I wiped it off with the back of my hand.

The world around me faded away when I caught up to my siblings. They were moving much slower than before. They had used too much of their element; they were physically weakened. As they were about to exit I stood between them and the door. Mother's head hung low with her eyes closed. I pointed my weapon at Valac's throat and said, "You're not taking her anywhere."

"Please don't do this, Rowan." Selene begged, tears ready to release. "She's your Mother."

Her plea made my soul ache. Selene had been the one sibling I had a decent relationship with. She didn't take up for me as I was being punished, but she refused to watch me suffer—unlike Valac. If she were stronger, she might have helped. But she was afraid. "After what she did to me, how can you ask me to step aside?"

Valac gripped a knife in his side pocket. "Get out of our way!" he shouted.

Just as I was about to respond Mother came to life, lunging at me. There was no time to think as the adrenaline kicked in. I pulled back on my sword, spun around for momentum, and carved the edge of the blade through her midsection, nearly cutting her in two. Her screams echoed through the room as she fell first to her knees, then onto her hip as she hit the floor. Selene dropped next to her, placing Mother's head in her lap. Valac stood motionless.

"How could you, Rowan?" Selene wailed, tears streaming down blood spattered cheeks.

I stared at the blood on the edge of my sword. My hand shook until I dropped the weapon at my side. It crashed to the ground next to me. Blood pooled all around Selene and Mother. As she took her final breath, cold reality set in: I'd killed my own Mother. I was no better than her. I was a monster. I tried to inhale a long breath, but could only manage short, intermittent puffs. I was hyperventilating.

"I'm going to kill you," Valac shrieked, pulling me out of my thoughts.

Before he could make a move someone grabbed him from behind. It was Jarrod, the lead air court knight. Valac tried to wrestle his way free with little success. I glanced around—we were surrounded by a slew of knights. They pulled my sister off of our Mother as she pleaded to stay with her. My chest tightened as I watched. At some point her body had caught fire. Soon, she'd be nothing more than a pile of ash.

I was still too numb to speak, even as an air court knight escorted me back to the front of the room. Taron was back on his throne taking in the room. He didn't have to say a word; it was written all over his face: shock and horror. Fire elemental corpses were collected and thrown into a burning heap. The air was thick from the fumes. Participating fire elementals who had survived were captured and put in iron chains. Air elementals cried over the dead bodies of their kin. Each watched helplessly as they crumbled into dry matter, floating away into the skies.

Liana appeared next to me, protected by two Gabriel Hounds in their animal form. She wrapped her arms around my neck. "Are you all right?"

I wasn't sure I could answer the question. Mother was dead. My siblings had organized a coup, costing many elementals their lives. Had they succeeded, it would have started an all-out war. "Were you part of this, Liana?"

"No. Valac told me they weren't coming. Had I known, I would have stopped them. Prisma is my sister, but I don't agree with what she did. I had only just found out what happened to you." She leaned as if she was trying to get a look at my back, I shifted away before she could. I wanted to believe her, but I didn't trust anyone anymore.

Liana backed away as air elementals brought my siblings forward.

Held by several guardians, they were made to stand next to me. Both wore iron cuffs on their hands and feet. Valac struggled to break free while Selene stayed silent, seemingly overwhelmed with grief. Taron's eyes travelled between them. His lips pressed together into a tight, thin line. I could only imagine what he was thinking.

I surprised myself when I stepped forward. "Please have mercy on them, King Taron."

His eyebrows rose. "Mercy? They are responsible for all the death you see before you. How can you ask this of me?"

"My mother is the reason we are all here, and now, she is dead." A vision of her body collapsing to the ground flashed in my head. I wasn't sure what I was feeling. All I sensed was emptiness, as if I'd been gutted. There was nothing left inside me. "Hasn't there been enough death for one day?"

Taron glared at me, his expression pained. Without words, I sensed his sympathy for my situation. "I am indebted to you for the enormous sacrifice you made to save my daughter. For that reason alone, I will show mercy on your siblings." He turned his attention to them. "You are hereby exiled from Avalon. You will live out your final days in the mortal world."

He wasn't giving them much mercy. Forcing them out of Avalon meant they would no longer be protected by the veil. They would both be dead in a matter of weeks. During the process their bodies and their power would weaken. The rapid changes would be excruciating. "This is your mercy?" Valac interjected. "We'd be better off if you killed us now."

"Remove them from my sight," Taron ordered, waving his arm. Jarrod, his lead knight, took hold of their shackles, pulling them toward one of the doors.

Then it hit me: Taron was sending them back to the mortal world where Kalin would be for another year. They were angry about Mother's death along with their own exile. A cold shiver ran down my spine as the door shut behind them. Taron didn't know Valac the way I did. As angry as he was, I have no idea what he might do. No, I couldn't let this happen. "Your Majesty, I wouldn't trust them in the mortal world. There's a good chance they might seek revenge."

He glared at the exit door, his eyes in small slits. "They will begin to weaken the moment they set foot in the mortal world. Soon, they will be helpless. They're no danger to anyone."

I couldn't believe what I was hearing. After everything he witnessed, he still didn't see the danger. Was it because the courts had been at peace for so long? Did he really believe no one else would break the laws of the decrees? Tension built in my shoulders. "How can you be so sure of that?"

Taron crossed his arms. He was irritated, I was questioning his decisions. "There will be additional knights around her home and also with her when she leaves. I have complete faith in her safety."

I wasn't sure what to say. It was clear he wouldn't be talked out of his decision. He believed in his knights. But I saw first-hand how easily Kalin was able to slip away when I watched her at school. I could have easily killed her if I hadn't come to my senses.

"The fire court cannot go without leadership. As unsavory as the current circumstances are, we must proceed with the coronation," King Taron announced.

"No!" I said, my voice so stern I hardly recognized it. I couldn't accept the crown. That would mean staying in Avalon. Valac would have plenty of time to devise a plan and rally other fire elementals to his cause. If Taron refused to see the danger, I wouldn't stand by and watch it happen. He healed me when I was brought to his castle. I wasn't a member of his court, or under his protection, so he could have let me die if he wanted to. I owe him my life. Even if it meant walking away from the throne, I would not allow my family to seek revenge against the air court.

I have to go back to the mortal world and protect Kalin.

"No?" Liana repeated, eyes widened with surprise.

She would never understand my decision. But, I was indebted to Taron. I had to keep his only daughter safe and prevent a war between the courts. Even though she would never see it, I was being a better king to them by protecting Kalin than I would if I counted on her knights to keep her safe. "I can't accept the crown."

"After everything, you'd abandon your own kin?" Liana asked.

I couldn't tell her my true reason. There were surviving fire elementals in chains who could hear every word of our conversation. If I gave them the impression Kalin was vulnerable, they might get word to others loyal to my mother. I wouldn't give them motivation to go after her. As much as it would break me I had to say, "I am no longer part of the fire court."

Fire ignited in her hands, racing up her arms. The hounds cowered at her side. "Not part of our court?" she asked, venom in her voice. "You're nothing but a deserter. You don't deserve the crown."

Her words burned a hole in my chest. After I was brutalized I didn't think any of them were worth saving. But maybe what they needed was a strong leader. Right now, that person wasn't me. I couldn't give them what they need until the threat was gone. I had to protect my court from war, even if it meant I was a deserter in their eyes. "I abdicate my throne to Liana. With her in power the crown shall remain with the House of Djin."

Taron leaned forward. "Rowan, are you sure this is what you want?"

I didn't see a choice. If my siblings attacked I would be there to stop them. I would do what I had to do to prevent a war. To protect Kalin. This was the only way. "Yes."

As I headed toward the exit, Liana shouted, "You'll never set foot in the fire territory again!"

If that was the sacrifice I had to make, I would accept it.

CHAPTER ELEVEN

Ten months had passed since I walked out of Taron's throne room. I had managed to stay undetected in the shadows while I watched over Kalin. Occasionally I ran into a fire elemental who kept me up to date with our court activities. I hadn't seen my siblings since their exile, which was for the best. I had heard they died months ago, but I decided to remain in the mortal world. I wasn't ready to return to Avalon. I might never be. Even if I was, where would I go?

I had turned down Taron's offer to become one of his knights. I told him I planned to keep guard over Kalin. He assured me she was safe, but something in my heart told me she wasn't. Although he didn't believe she was in danger he didn't stop me. Part of me believed he wanted me to protect her, but he would never admit it. He was the last person I saw before I left Avalon.

In the mortal world, I'd become a solitary—an elemental not associated with any of the courts. Rejecting my court should have meant losing my connection with the fire element, but I was still considered part of the ruling family. That meant some of my power remained. I could still summon the fire element, but the level of power I used to have was lessened. I needed to stay strong in other ways to combat this weakness. When I wasn't tailing Kalin I spent my time weapons training. I worked with swords, knives, and throwing stars. Anything I could get my hands on.

The extra time in the mortal world did have one advantage. Aging another year had gotten rid of all my baby fat. My shoulders had widened and my muscles had mass. Thanks to the daily sword training, my body had morphed; I had become a lethal weapon.

During the long periods of loneliness my thoughts often returned to Marcus. He hadn't resurfaced. I feared our friendship was over for good. I assumed he'd been assigned to another high-ranking elemental. I was sickened when I imagined him in that position, but I had made the right decision. Although I was sure Marcus wasn't happy, he would agree Kalin needed saving to prevent a war between the courts.

The elements must always stay in balance.

When I returned from my evening training sessions I was surprised to see activity in Kalin's house. All the lights were on. At least ten air elementals moved in and out of the house in a hurry. When I saw two of them heading into the forest I followed. After about two miles, they approached an area cloaked by a glamour. Soon after, Jarrod stepped out of a portal, handing them royal robes. After some conversation he returned through the pathway.

I thought about how much time had passed since I left Avalon. Kalin must have been approaching her birthday. It was time for her to return to her father. Relief spilled over my shoulders. Taron's daughter would return to him unharmed and I could finally let go of my fear of war. It felt like a victory on so many levels. As the guards returned to Kalin's house I followed far enough behind not to be seen.

I was looking forward to seeing the Princess one last time before—

Out of the corner of my eye I saw a flash in the distance. My eyes roamed the area, trying to locate the tiny blimp. The trees were so thick they blocked most of the moonlight. It was almost impossible to see anything far away. Just as I started to head in the direction of the light I heard a pained scream.

I whirled around.

The two air knights were being attacked: one was engulfed in flames, the other trying to fight two fire elementals at once. I ran full speed toward them releasing my sword from its sheath. As I got closer I recognized the female fire elemental—Malin. I had heard she was appointed the leader of Liana's personal guard. Why did Liana send them to attack? There hasn't been a quarrel between their courts since I'd been here.

I threw a baseball size ball of fire at the back of the male fire elemental. It wouldn't hurt him, but it would draw his attention away. When he turned around, the air knight used his wind magic to suffocate him by sucking the air out of his lungs. Malin saw what was happening and slid a knife across his neck. A river of blood ran down his shirt as he collapsed onto the ground.

Dammit.

Sometime during the struggle the air knight on fire had stopped screaming. It appeared he was already dead. While the male fire elemental caught his breath,

Malin came at me. I had almost reached them when she shot a stream of fire in my direction, missing me by only inches. As she pulled out a sword I went straight for her. Our weapons clashed, screeching.

"Why did Liana send you, Malin?" I demanded.

I pushed into her, forcing her back a foot or two. We circled each other. "What do we have here?" Malin asked. "If it isn't the deserter of our court."

As we moved, I realized her partner had disappeared. A twig broke, and in one quick motion, I reversed my grip on the blade and plunged it behind me. There was a gasp, then silence. I found her friend. I pulled my sword out, letting him fall to the ground.

Malin had already put a good distance between us when I asked, "I'm only going to ask you one more time. Why did Liana send you?" My voice sounded more like a growl.

She surprised me by throwing an iron spear. It hit me in my side, burning my skin instantly. I fell to my knees, and when I looked up, she was gone. As I pulled the spear out with my bare hand the skin on my palm charred. My mind raced wondering why they had attacked out of nowhere when it had been peaceful for more than a year.

The blood in my veins turned cold. "Kalin!"

KEEP READING
FOR A SNEAK PEEK OF

BOOK ONE:
MORTAL ENCHANTMENT

MORTAL ENCHANTMENT: CHAPTER ONE

I wonder if I can get pizza in Avalon?

My life was about to change in every conceivable way and I was thinking about my menu options. I rolled my eyes. It was time to get serious. Today was the big day. My last day in the mortal world for who knows how long. But most importantly, the last time I would see my mother. No matter how many times I begged, she refused to come with me. She insisted my dad needed time alone with me. Father/daughter bonding type stuff.

But that was the deal they made even before I was born. I got to spend my childhood with my mother, then once I turned sixteen I'd move to Avalon to be with my father—the elemental king of the air court.

As far as my friends were concerned I was moving to Paris. I bragged about how I'd be living in the most romantic city in the world, surrounded by cute European guys with sexy French accents. My throat tightened up each time they told me how jealous they were. They had no idea how miserable I felt lying to them. Or how I envied their freedom.

But, it wasn't all bad.

Moving to Avalon meant I could get to know my father. We had gotten close through his visits into my dreams, but it wasn't the same as actually having him in my physical life. Plus, and this was a big plus, I'd be a princess in the air court where Dad planned to teach me to control the air element and weather magic.

A knock on my bedroom door startled me out of my thoughts.

Mom stepped inside. Most days she wore lounge t-shirts and relaxed pants, but today, she had on a canary yellow sweater and skinny jeans. Sometimes I forgot how beautiful she is. Because of our red wavy hair and fair complexion, many people had mistaken us for sisters. I swear, the woman never aged. I watched as her green eyes roamed the room. "Kalin, you haven't packed a thing."

Dad told me he would send additional knights to retrieve whatever I wanted, but what was the point? I doubted my collection of *Pez* dispensers or assorted sets of cartoon pajamas would be acceptable possessions of an elemental princess. "I wasn't sure what to bring. I mean, it's not like we've done much traveling."

I regretted the words as soon as they came out. Judging by her face, I'd say they stung a little. It wasn't her fault we'd stayed in one place. Mom was always worried that I might be in danger. I never understood why, especially since we had always lived with my father's knights surrounding our house and following me everywhere I went. Knights who were annoying, never giving me any privacy.

"Are you nervous?" she asked.

"No." I was scared out of my mind. I didn't know what to expect. Besides my father and his knights, I had never met another elemental. I worried if they would like me or if I would make any friends. Also, I wondered what it would be like to date an elemental. Did elementals date? These were questions I didn't feel comfortable asking my dad.

I couldn't ask my mom either. These last few weeks had been tough on her. She had known I would be leaving, but it was hard for her to let me go. It was hard for me too. I had never spent a day of my life without her. I wish I could understand why she wouldn't come with me. Anytime I asked about her relationship with my father she found a way to change the subject.

"What are you going to wear?"

I looked down at my black hoodie and jeans. "I guess I should wear something nice, right?"

She clasped her hands on my shoulders. "No, you should wear what you want. Your Dad will be ecstatic to see you regardless."

I had to try one last time before I go. She might finally open up to me. I put my hands around her wrists so she couldn't escape. "I'm sure he'd like to see you too. Why won't you come with me?"

She leaned her forehead into mine. "It's complicated."

I let go of her, heading toward a pile of folded clothes on my bed. As I inserted them into my backpack, I said, "That's what you always say."

"Look, I promise you, one day we'll sit down and talk about it. But today is about you."

I grabbed the picture of us off my nightstand and placed it inside the backpack. "If you never come to Avalon, I may never see you again."

A second later she was next to me. I turned to face her as she said, "I didn't say I'd never come. I said not right now. Your Dad has been waiting a long time for you. He deserves your full attention."

"And what about what I deserve? What I want? Did you even think about that when you both sat down and planned out my future?" I snapped.

Her eyebrows furrowed. "Are you saying you don't want to go?"

I wasn't sure. I had always known what they had planned for me so I never really thought about what I wanted. It wasn't until my friends started talking about their college plans that I began to resent the idea. Yet, there was a big part of me that wanted to go. "All I'm saying is it would've been nice to have a choice."

Her eyes watered. "I'm sorry, Kalin. It's just—"

I cut her off. "Complicated, I know." Guilt burned in my chest. The last thing I wanted was to fight with her on our last day together. "Let's forget about it for now. Like you said, you will tell me when it's the right time."

She hugged me. "Exactly."

I held on, not wanting to let her go. "I'm going to miss you so much."

Sniffling, she replied, "I'm going to miss you too."

Okay, I needed to get out of here before we both broke into the ugly cry. I grabbed my backpack and slid it over my shoulder. "I'm going to go wait outside for the knights to return."

She wiped her tears away with the sleeve of her sweater. "I'll wait with you."

"No, if you're there it's only going to be that much harder to leave." I hugged her again. "Goodbye, Mom. I love you so much."

"I love you too. Be careful."

I winked. "I always am."

Once I finally made it outside, the frigid midnight breeze stung my face. I slung my backpack over my shoulder and locked the backdoor. I was instructed to wait here for my father's knights to return. They should have been back by now. I decided it didn't matter, I didn't need them. The forest behind my house went back about two miles, but I knew every inch. As a child I'd spent hours wandering the dirt walkways pretending to be on a treasure hunt with my friends. I had also kissed my first boyfriend behind one of the larger oak trees on the edge of our backyard.

The weathered wooden planks of the back porch creaked with each step. I plunked down three stairs and headed straight for the dark forest. When I reached the entrance of the woodland, I turned around and took one last look at the home I grew up in. The modest brick rancher sat alone in a tucked away cul-de-sac. It was so hidden it didn't even show up on a standard GPS. I knew that had to be a selling point for Mom.

She preferred quiet, tucked away spaces over city life.

I swallowed the lump in my throat and made my way into the dim woods. The scent of wet moss filled my nostrils. I hiked at least a mile before I stopped to get my bearings. The moonlight did little to illuminate the forest floor, it had become nearly impossible to see anything more than a few feet in front of me. The overriding silence made me shiver. Reality check: I was in the middle of the woods, in the dark, with no idea how to find Dad's knights.

I should've waited—

A familiar white shimmer appeared in the distance. Even though I had spent my entire childhood in the mortal world, Dad had sent me books about the history of the elementals. From the reading I knew the brightness I saw was a pathway; the fastest way to travel to Avalon. There were hidden paths all over the mortal world, but only elementals could see them.

Someone had just arrived.

I called out, letting them know where I was, but got no response. The light thinned until I could only see a shadow heading in my direction. Once she was a few feet in front of me, her creamy porcelain skin, slightly oversized amber eyes, and feathered wings came into view. From far away I had assumed she was one of my father's knights, but her black feathers left no question about of her identity.

She was a fire elemental.

The fire court drew their power from the Earth's core. They controlled everything from a volcano eruption down to a simple burning match. From the stories I read, I learned they were passionate and unpredictable much like their element.

I bit the inside of my cheek to hide the excited grin trying to form across my face. For a second I thought about asking her to ignite a flame from her palm like the ones I'd seen in pictures, but I didn't want to come off like a moron. Minus her wings, she might have passed for a mortal in her strapless forest green tube top and dark colored jeans. The round onyx pendant embedded in silver wings around her neck was unusual, as was the twisted grin across her face.

"Taron's a fool to leave you unattended." Her voice

was calm, almost soothing, as she circled around me. "It's truly a disappointment how easy this will be."

A consuming sense of unease crept from my scalp to my toes. "What's a disappointment?"

Her hand shot out, clutched my neck, and raised me off the ground. My feet dangled and I gasped for air as I tried to make sense out of what was happening. Why would she want to attack me? Panic gagged me as I clawed feverishly at her hands, digging my fingernails into her skin.

"Are you really this helpless?" she laughed.

"Let me go," I demanded, trying to sound intimidating even though I was confused and filled with fear. I grimaced as her grip tightened.

She thrust my body into the nearest tree and pain radiated up my spine. Had I been only mortal, she might have broken my back. Still in shock I tried to twist away, scraping my forearm against a broken tree limb. She smirked, her hand remaining clutched around my neck. "You are in no position to order me around, girl!"

Whatever this was, it was beyond bad.

"Get away from her!" a deep voice shouted.

My attacker peered over her shoulder and her grip loosened. "Back for more, deserter?" she asked, her voice coated with venom.

Deserter?

While her attention was somewhere else, I thrust my knee into her stomach and fell to the ground. She scooped me up by my shirt, pressing my back into her chest with her fingers wrapped tightly around my neck. I drew blood when I clawed my fingernails into her hands but she didn't even wince.

A flash of silver light whizzed by my head and my

captor's grip eased. This time I was able to slip away. I stumbled. Reaching out to steady myself, I only found air and crashed onto the ground. She launched herself at me again and ended up straddled on top of me with one hand clasped around my windpipe. My lungs burned for air. Legs thrashing, I tried to wiggle free. Yet, throughout my efforts, she showed no sign of strain. Her other hand pulled shards of what I assumed was iron from her neck.

Blackness filled the rim of my vision. Frantically I searched the ground for a rock, but found nothing. I plunged my hand into the damp forest floor. Maybe a little dirt in her eyes would give me enough time—

He emerged out of the shadows, thrusting a large knife into her back. She arched upwards in pain, releasing me from her grasp. I rolled onto my side gasping for air in between coughs. Hearing a struggle behind me, I took a glimpse over my shoulder. The male elemental lodged another silver blade into her back before she could crawl away.

"Go!" he yelled.

Several yards away the moonlight illuminated a clearing. I got to my feet and ran towards it. By the time I reached a large row of bushes, I ached all over. *What the hell?* Since when did the fire court want me dead? I mean, she was definitely trying to kill me. In all the chaos of the last several minutes, that was the one thing I was sure of. No way had she thought I was someone else. It was clear she knew who I was and where I'd be.

A throbbing ache drew my attention to a cut on my forearm. It was swollen and dripping blood. I tore off a piece of the bottom of my shirt, wrapping it around the wound. Peering through the leaves, I watched my attacker thrash violently on the ground. The male elemental tore the necklace from her neck, then faster than I could blink, he slit her throat. Black blood spurted from her neck and onto his shirt. He jumped out of the way when her body ignited in flames and watched until all that was left of her was a pile of ash.

My rescuer stepped into the clearing. I caught his stare and slowly rose to my feet. At my measly 5'3", I guessed he was close to a foot taller and maybe seventeen or eighteen. His brown shaggy hair hung in waves over his eyes, the silver barbell in his eyebrow shimmered in the moonlight. A torn blue t-shirt showed off his lean, muscular build.

His appearance suggested he had spent a lot of time in the mortal world. For every young elemental, years away from Avalon were necessary. There was no other way to mature into adulthood. The magical veil that kept Avalon hidden from the rest of the world also prevented anyone inside from aging.

Adrenaline raced through my veins. "Who was she?" My voice shook.

He glanced down at the necklace in his hand. "She was an assassin from the fire court."

My brain had officially left my body. "There has to be some kind of mistake." In all the nights Dad had visited with me in my dreams, he never once mentioned any tension between the air and fire courts. I thought the elementals were at peace. "She must have been after someone else."

He put the necklace in his jeans pocket and shot me

a stern look. "The dead air court elementals she killed would prove otherwise."

His words burned into me like a branding iron. They died because of me. Guilt rushed over me as I imagined the loss their families would feel. "You're sure she killed them?" I knew I had heard him correctly, but for some reason, I needed to hear it again.

"Yes. I found them only a short distance away from the pathway."

If my attacker went to the pathway first, she must have been expecting me to be there. Oh god, this was getting worse by the second. "Wait. How do I know this isn't some kind of trick? How do I know you're not working with her?" I took a few steps backwards to put some distance between us. "How do I know *you* didn't kill them?"

"The fact that you're alive is a pretty good indication that I'm not trying to kill you."

He pulled up the bottom of his shirt and wiped the black blood off his cheek. The curve of his hip was exposed and I forced myself to look away. I needed to focus, not drool over some guy who was obviously dangerous.

"What's your name?" I asked.

"Rowan."

"Were you tracking her?"

"No."

Rowan definitely wasn't big on details. "Then, what are you doing here?"

"I was in the area." He looked away and I got the feeling he was hiding something. "Taron has knights at your house. You should be there instead of scampering around in the forest."

I crossed my arms. "I wasn't *scampering*." I got impatient and stupidly decided I could find my own way to the pathway.

"Whatever you want to call it doesn't change the fact that you're alone and unprotected." The leaves rustled, and Rowan tensed. "We have to get you out of here."

He looped his arm inside mine and towed me deeper into the dark forest. I had to jog to keep up. His urgency put my already amped up suspicions into epic overdrive. "Why? Where are you taking me?"

"You're not safe here. The elemental who attacked you wasn't the only one they sent. There could be others."

"This is insane!" Pulling back on my arm, I forced him to stop. "I'm not taking another step until you tell me who you are and what's going on."

"Look, this wasn't the way this was supposed to go down. I was supposed to be done, and now—" He cut himself off, emitting a low growl. "Trust me, this isn't going to make the highlight reel for me either."

His answer only confused me more. "You were done with what? You're not making any sense."

"You, I meant," he snarled. "You and your... situation."

"Wow, and up until now, I thought you were part of the welcoming party." My *situation*? What was this guy's damage? He doesn't even know me. And who said I invited him to be part of my *situation* anyway?

He took a deep breath, then exhaled as if he'd been defeated in a battle. "I killed two fire court assassins to protect you. Now, I have no choice. I have to return to Avalon and tell the council what happened."

Finally, Mister Personality said something I understood. The council was judge and jury to everything. The members included the four royal families and several other high ranking elementals. I definitely wasn't convinced I could trust Rowan, but Dad was a member of the council. If that was where he planned to go, then it's exactly where I needed to be. "I'm coming with you."

"Absolutely not." He shook his head. "We need to go back to your mother's house. The knights can take you somewhere safe until I can get this mess sorted out."

I let out an exaggerated breath. "Listen, I really appreciate what you did back there—I really do, but I need to find my father. If you want to keep me safe, take me to the council."

"Last time I checked, the fire court was part of the council." He pointed over his shoulder. "I think the big pile of ash back there sent a pretty clear message."

He wasn't wrong, but I had reached my limit. "Okay, let me make this simple for you. You'll either take me to the council, or I'll scream my freakin' head off until I alert every elemental within a five mile distance." I poked my finger into his chest, which was surprisingly hard. "Do you understand me now?"

With his hands balled into fists at his sides, he said, "Fine, whatever. Walk right into danger if you insist, but don't say I didn't warn you."

He pressed his palms into the air and the blackness rippled like ocean waves. We must have been standing close to the glamour protecting the pathway. Elementals used glamour magic to change the appearance of an object or to hide something from view.

A howl cried out strong enough to shake the ground, we fought to stay on our feet.

"What the hell is that?" I shrieked.

"Gabriel Hounds, which means we're officially out of time." In one swift motion, he wrapped his arms around me and hurtled us into the dark current.

Want to read more? *Mortal Enchantment* will be available for purchase on May 20, 2014! Add *Mortal Enchantment* to your GoodReads TBR!

ACKNOWLEDGMENTS

There have been so many people who have helped me throughout my journey. The first in a long line are my parents, Russell and Brenda Howell. Your love, encouragement, and support have been priceless. I feel so lucky to be your daughter. I want to send out some love to my brother, Michael Howell. You believed this could happen even before I did. Thank you, little bro. None of this would be possible without my husband, Christopher. The fact that I found a man as wonderful as you still astonishes me every day. Thank you for putting a ring on it. My life wouldn't be complete without my daughter, Madison. I didn't truly understand the depth of love until you came into the world. Everything I do is for you, sweet girl. This novella doesn't exist without Courtney Koschel. You're the best editor and friend a person could wish for. I've had many editors, critique partners, and beta readers throughout my writing career. These people are amazeballs: Jessica Reigle, Janice Foy, Vanessa Barger, Jennifer Sipes, Bob Havey, Camille Morales, Jordan Mierek, Heather Howland, Kerry Vail, Jen McKinnon Scicchitano, Cathy Yardley, Will Kalif and Kristin Anders. Each of you has helped me grow as a writer and I want you to know I am truly grateful for all that you have given me. Special thanks to Jennifer L. Armentrout for lots of reasons.

Mostly, thanks for thinking this was a good idea and for being full of awesome. Last, but not least, I want to thank you—the reader. Thank you for giving me a chance. This series has been a labor of love and I truly appreciate your support. Big, awkward virtual hug coming your way. ;-)

ABOUT THE AUTHOR

Stacey O'Neale lives in Annapolis, Maryland. When she's not writing, she spends her time fangirling over books, blogging, watching fantasy television shows, cheering for the Baltimore Ravens, and hanging out with her husband and daughter.

Her career in publishing started as a blogger-turned-publicist for two successful small publishers. Stacey writes young adult paranormal romance and adult science fiction romance. Her books always include swoon-worthy heroes, snarky heroines, and lots of kissing.

Stacey loves hearing from readers. Follow her on Twitter @StaceyONeale, look for her on Facebook, Pinterest, and GoodReads. You can also visit her blog at http://staceyoneale.com/.

Made in the USA
Charleston, SC
04 October 2014